Falling in Stilettos

"What if one day you
woke up and your life wasn't
as you remembered it?"

Jeneth Blackert

FALLING IN STILETTOS
BY JENETH BLACKERT

Published by:

Also by Jeneth Blackert

Seven Dragons: A guide to a limitless mind

Simple Marketing: The simple way to big business growth

Seminars by Jeneth Blackert

Crazy Rich & Free to Be
www.crazyrichfree.com

Find Jeneth online and receive a free training at:

www.jeneth.com

Gratitude

I would like to express my gratitude to the following contributors of this book.

Joe Blackert – Thank you for being the love of my life and being right there with me for endless hours of brainstorming.

The Jeneth, LLC Team – I couldn't create so dynamically without you – thanks to Lyanca Reyna, Deborah Hawkins and Carole Magouirk.

Heather Govenor – I'm so grateful for your edits. Your contribution has truly supported this creation with ease.

Dr. Dain Heer – Thank you for showing me there is a different way to be in this world.

1

Waking Up

WHERE IS IT? C'MON. I fumble around the soft yet unfamiliar bed sheets. I know it's here somewhere. My cell phone shrills again, and I jolt fully awake.

I start my usual morning orientation process asking questions. Okay Rachael think, think! Where am I? What happened? What time is it? I take a deep breath and look around. Who is he? My eyes drift across the room and rest on a thirty-something-year-old man peeking at me from above his newspaper. I swivel around in shock.

Okay. Think. The previous night's adventure begins to rumble around in my head. Something about dancing, a bar, actor-slash-bartender—Oh yes, Ashton.

"Good morning," he says casually. Mmmm. He's cute. He has a sexy scruff beard and beaming eyes. OMG. Yummy. Tingles run through my spine. When I first spotted him last night I told Katie, my best friend, that he was totally cute

1

and I would totally go out with him if I were single. And we both know the truth is I don't ever break up, I trade up.

I giggle inwardly when I remember Katie staring in amazement as Ashton grabbed a glass from the bar, rolled it down his arm and flipped a drink in it. I knew she wanted him. But I *got* him. It's important to be with someone that other people want.

Katie has been my best friend since we met at the neighborhood pool when we were both seven. Katie made quite an impression that summer when she dropped an ice cream cone on my brand new pink polka-dot bikini and managed to include my beautiful matching flip flops. Thereafter, this became an endearing behavior of hers. Whenever I find myself ready to be in the spotlight, she's always ready to embarrass me with some "Katie-prone" mishap—which I appreciate because it always makes me look good.

Last night at The Seven Grand Bar was no different. I couldn't believe her. As I took the cherry out of my Manhattan and allowed it to tumble on my lips in a flirting gesture towards Ashton, Katie took off her jacket and in so doing bumped my drink enough for it to splash all over my brand new white cotton BCBG skintight dress. Grrr—

Once when we were rollerblading she literally ran into this gorgeous guy. He fell and she fell smack on top of him. The poor victim is my current fiancé, Jake, who I'm sure is the one calling me right now. Where is that silly little phone?

I feel another little tickle running up and down my spine as I look at Ashton with my "cute-eye-stare." Ashton is what most people refer to as tall, dark and handsome. And although he looks fantastic, as I remember the details of last night I find myself irresistibly attracted to who he is. I love his fun humor and how he can relish in every single moment. I remember watching as he savored life, from tumbling the food around in his mouth to dancing to the hip music at the night club. He seems really comfortable in his skin.

Already, being with him makes me feel unique, playful, more expressed and just plain the real me. I can't put my finger on exactly how or why. It's really refreshing to sense that I'm with someone who doesn't pretend to be someone he's not. This is something I am completely unfamiliar with. I have always pretended to be someone I'm not. I have never really felt accepted, worthy or good enough in my life. My father always put me in my place, telling me the many ways I was wrong.

Last night, when Ashton asked me to dinner, I did my best to remain dispassionate and calm, even though a huge smile kept breaking through. It always feels so amazing to be wanted, but I didn't want him to know how deeply I desired him. I know to wait until I am sure a man likes me before I make any move.

We went to one of the finest Italian restaurants in Beverly Hills, where he ordered the most expensive bottle of wine the menu had to offer. I know this because I was looking at the wine menu wondering which wine he would choose for us. Typically, my dates order the cheapest crap on the menu, which irritates the hell out of me. It was an amazing feeling to be treated with the best.

As we toasted our first glass, he asked me question after question about myself and my life. I have to admit, it was wonderful to feel like someone cared about what I said and was actually listening to me. After several glasses of wine we found ourselves unable to stop laughing. I felt completely uninhibited and free for the first time ever in my life. Yes, I said it! For the first time ever in my life. So, when Ashton asked me about the things that move me, I confided in him my secret dream of becoming a celebrity shoe designer—a secret I've hidden and kept highly guarded since I was sixteen when I realized I was obsessively passionate about shoes—and why I believe shoes are gateways to our infinite being. He really understood me. When you can say "gateway to infinite being" and talk about being moved and what moves you beyond the physical form, you know you've met someone cool.

He asked me why I was hiding such a beautiful secret. I shrugged and told him that I don't like to think of myself as a dreamer because dreamers seem to always have their heads in the clouds. I have to admit his response caught me by utter surprise: "But Rachael, aren't you a dreamer? Isn't that who you are? What is true to you? Are you really willing to deny that about yourself?"

I simply shrugged, but I have to admit it got me thinking, as I had never quite thought of it that way.

When Reese Witherspoon entered the restaurant, she acknowledged Ashton with a little wave. He suavely and deliberately gestured back, and that's when my interrogation began. I started with some simple questions: Why do you live in LA? What do you do for a living? And, of course, the obvious question: How do you know Reese? His answers were plain and simple. He's a producer and actor. She's in the industry. When I asked what he does for fun, he answered with one word: "Everything." I continued probing with quirky facial gestures, and finally his face creased up with amusing laughter.

"Look, I know it's different. You see, several years ago I made a conscious choice to be me—no matter what—and change, clear anything that is keeping me from knowing and being me. So, today, I live in all choice. I choose to really live in each moment and only do what's fun for me. So I look for stories that move me that I may want to produce. I practice for roles, which I also love. I ski. I dance. I play. I go out with people I enjoy being with. I have fun." Then he humbly smiled and shrugged.

My thoughts became stuck on one word that came out of his mouth. So, I stupidly said, "Dance? You like to dance? What type of dance? I love to dance." I knew that I could impress him with my modern dance style.

He smiled warmly and said, "Great! Then that's what we'll do next." He gulped down the last swig of his wine and asked to be excused from the table.

I nodded and watched him confidently stride towards Reese's table. Once he arrived I willed myself not to spy on him. Instead I redirected my eyes and stared down my empty wine glass while I calibrated my "drunken" level. I declared it to be a four on a scale of one to ten: one being completely sober and ten being throwing-up-in-the-toilet drunk. This was probably higher than it should have been on any first date. But, of course this was not a date—I mean, I'm engaged, I reminded myself with a heap of guilt.

A few minutes later Ashton returned, "Reese thought you were Jennifer Lawrence," he smiled. "Would you like to meet her? Or are you ready to hit the club?"

I nervously jumped, "A quick hello sounds nice." As I stood, Ashton placed his hand on the small of my back and my body quivered all over. We stopped to greet Reese and then walked to the parking lot that way; I loved the feel of the subtle connection. As the valet trotted off to get the car, Ashton dropped me into a full dancing dip.

Once we arrived at the nearby dance club, I knew within seconds that Ashton was an expert dancer. Despite feeling diminished by my lack of expertise, he twirled me so spectacularly I ended the evening feeling like a modern Cinderella at the ball. I expected to lose a slipper or have the BMW turn into a pumpkin, but it was just awesome. I hid a giggle with this thought until he asked me what I was smiling about, and when I told him he replied, "That would be the perfect name for your shoe company: Cinderella." He had said it so seriously that it caught me by surprise. This was probably the first time someone actually acknowledged my dream as a feasible reality. This stumbled around in my head for a moment, and while I looked for a half-intelligent response, I burped. Not just a little burp, but one so large and loud that it caused others to turn and look. I placed a hand over my mouth and shuddered with embarrassment.

"I'm sorry," I whispered as I watched his face break into a big amusing smile that escalated us both into tummy-rolling laughter.

* * *

Under the sheets, I give a full body stretch and I can tell my stomach hurts from laughing all night long, but the other specifics are somewhat of a blur, and I have to admit, I can't stop smiling.

Let's see, I remember Katie being furious when I started to flirt with Ashton. I longed for her approval, which I knew I wouldn't get. She thinks my fiancé Jake, a recent UCLA Law School graduate, is good for me. And he is. Jake and I have been dating nearly three years. We met that day rollerblading when Katie smashed into him. Katie and Jake had exchanged information and kept in-touch. I was re-introduced to him over dinner a month later. Actually, I had thought she liked him, but she let him ask me out that night.

I think of Jake as this good-looking, clean-cut, responsible catch. Everyone wants him, but he loves me. And Jake *is* good for me. At least I think he's good for me. I mean, he keeps me grounded and in control and that's a good thing, right? He's also amazing on paper. He graduated magna cum laude and has been recruited by law firms across the globe, so I'm sure he will make a lot of money. We still haven't decided on a date for our upcoming wedding. There is something inside me that loves the idea of being engaged to the guy that everyone wants.

I peer through a wrinkle in the sheets and look at

Ashton. Although Jake is the guy everyone wants, he's not what Ashton is. Ashton is sexy and totally yummy. And not just in looks and physique, but his energy in all that he is, well, totally yummy. My body quivers as I stare at him through the sheets. Yes. Yummy.

Jake and I haven't agreed on a wedding date yet. The truth is, I may be avoiding the whole wedding date and marriage topic. Every time the subject comes up I avoid it. Last week when we were shopping, Jake wanted to stop at Pottery Barn to look for a couch for our new house—a house that his parents bought for him. I convinced him it would be far better to go clothes shopping. I mean, no one actually cares about the inside of your house, but everyone has an opinion about how you look—especially in LA. Despite getting my way, hostility cracked around him as he continued to talk about how we needed to plan. And despite moving my attention to designer shoes, I kept hearing Jake blurt out things like it'd be our first couch and how we can really make our house a home and blah, blah, blah. And suddenly my thoughts responded in a loud, heavy, NO. The truth is, the thought of "ours" makes my feet grow colder. In fact, whenever he mentions planning for the house or wedding, I always find hundreds of reasons as to why it's just too soon or the wrong time—whatever excuse I can come up with.

I gasp and nearly jump out from under the covers when my phone shrills again. Ashton lifts my stained white dress from the ground to uncover it. "Here it is," he says tossing it on the bed next to me.

I stare at it lifelessly. "Thanks," I say with frown.

Ashton meets my eyes and empathically matches my lifeless remorse. "We can find you a new dress," he trails off. I can tell he knows exactly what's wrong, and it's not the dress.

I shake my head in remorse and look down at my left ring finger with the missing engagement ring. A flood of mixed emotions are overwhelming my body. It starts with the guilt I have from not phoning Jake last night. I should have sent a text. I totally suck. I'm such a jerk. I look at the phone and then at Ashton. And then another emotion of total exhilaration delights me. Ashton is looking at me in a way that makes me feel totally seen. On the surface it's nice, but there's something inside me that makes me want to run and hide. I hunch my shoulders, flip the phone over and then say, "Nobody, important." My eyes meet his, and I know he knows I'm lying. "Fine. It's Jake. My ex." I reply to redeem myself. I can tell he still knows I'm lying. "Fine. It's Jake. My current. So. There," I say crossing my arms.

I gaze at him as he walks over to the bed and sits next to me.

"Hi," he says with a renewed smile. He pulls a piece of confetti from my hair. He shows me as he giggles, "Escapee from the club."

I blush and let out a little snort. I find myself smiling again reminiscing about last night. He's witty, charming, unpredictable, funny, sexy yet casual, deliberate, and I think I might be in love. No. I am in love. "Did you sleep well?" I ask because I don't know what else to say.

9

"Yes. I slept well," he responds, knowing I'm just making conversation and I'm actually paralyzed with nerves. "The real question is, how are you? Okay from last night?"

"Oh, yes, I'm good." I say seeing sunlight breaking through ceiling-length embroidered silk drapes behind him. I turn my head to observe my surroundings and catch a glimpse of the shiny marble countertops in his elaborate master bathroom. "So, where are we?" I finally ask, struggling to hide my nerves from my random thoughts. I consider the possible answers, and my heart starts pounding with fear. I am desperately curious. I mean this is an expensive house. I have a thought we are at his parents—then one about him purchasing it with an inheritance—then one about him being a drug dealer.

"We are at my house in Malibu. I'll take you for a tour later if you wish," he replies with delight.

"Did we?" I make a gesture with a circle and a pointer-finger.

"You don't remember?" he teases.

I shrug as if I don't, but I actually do remember.

"No, we didn't but we played. We really played. You don't remember?" Ashton asks jokingly.

I clasp my right hand to my forehead and drag it to the side of my face and giggle. "I just wanted to make sure *you* remembered."

"Sure you did," he says sarcastically. "And let me just say you give a good puppy re-enactment, by the way."

"That must have been sexy," I respond hiding under the sheets.

"Yes. Actually, it was very endearing." He dives under the covers to find me.

After a brief tickle fight, Ashton catches his breath and with a cute smile says, "Hey, why don't you shower so we can get outta here." He looks at my Manhattan-stained cotton dress on the floor, "And grab some clothes from my closet, my dear." He gestures grandly to the shower with both his arms.

"Okay," I reply as I cocoon myself with the flat sheet and place my feet on the cool wood floor.

I walk deliberately towards the master bath, and before I close the bathroom door I teasingly drop the sheet and slap my bottom looking to Ashton for a response. When I close the door I hear him chuckle.

I can't believe my eyes. I am staring at a twelve-head steam shower. My heart starts hammering and my mental chatter takes hold. Oh my goodness, I better get out of here. Who is this guy? Is he a drug dealer? A thief? What if I'm accessory to a crime? I gasp. What if he's in the mafia and I've been abducted? I have a sudden vision of my mug shot. Stop! I command my thoughts. Just take a shower. It's going to be just fine. I look at the shower knobs. Now, how does this thing work? I switch on one knob and water begins spraying the room. Damn. I let out a shriek.

"Is everything okay in there?" Ashton yells from the bedroom.

"Yes. Um, I'm fine. I'll be out soon," I sing back. Okay, Rachael, you can do this. I mean how hard can this be? I switch on the largest of the three knobs, and suddenly one of the flexible tubes begins looping in circles spraying even more water in the room. I screech and switch it off.

"Do you need help?" Ashton yells again. I can hear him giggling in the background.

"No. I think I've got it now," I yell back.

I study the knobs and nozzles. Let's see. If that goes with that and this goes with this, that means this one will go to—ah yes—I turn on the next knob. Finally, normal water comes out of the main spout. Good enough.

After my indulgent shower, I put on probably the softest white robe I have ever touched. I wring out my long brown locks and start detangling the snarls from our many twirls last night. I look in the full-length mirror and find an enormous closet gleaming behind me. I curiously pivot and walk directly in. There are hundreds of designer suits in a perfect line and some casual wear neatly folded on shelves to the side. I peek at a label: Giorgio Armani. Just for grins, I check another: Fred Segal. Alrighty then.

Then I see them. My jaw drops. My heart races and my blood pressure climbs. It's pure art. Varnished. Grosgrain. Laced. Leather soles. I see every single shoe Ashton wears. I'm in love.

I know without a shadow of a doubt that shoes reveal the secrets in our soul. Ashton's shoes say, "I am phenomenal. I am strong. I know who I am." While Jake's shoes say something like, "I care about education. I am professional, boring, and I don't care." Katie's shoes say, "I'm doing my best. I'm trying." Mine say, "Look at me! See me! I demand attention!" I have to admit, I would love it if one day my shoes would say, "I am amazing!"

I slip on a soft blue gray ringer tee shirt and a pair of light gray drawstring sweat pants. I peer at myself in the mirror. I give a little curtsy and to my horror I see Ashton behind me. My heart drops. Ashton is watching me in amusement. I turn. And now, he's giving me a standing ovation. I curtsy again towards him with blushing cheeks.

"Are you having fun?" He smiles and reaches his right hand behind my left ear and draws me in for a kiss.

"Why yes. I am. So, sue me." I say nodding with a flirty grin.

With a snicker he says, "Well, it's Sunday. Whatcha got planned?"

I stand there dumbfounded for a moment. Is he asking me out? Really? Hee. Hee. Hee. I tuck my chin and look up with flirty eyes, shrug my right shoulder and say, "Hmm, I don't think I have any plans. I'm not too much of a plan-ahead-girl." This is not entirely true. I mean, normally I would have plans with Jake. "Whatcha thinking?"

"Well, do you want to join me for an adventure today? I have a horseback riding trip planned down the beach and then an early dinner with some actor friends. Interested?"

My whole body and everything I am says, yes, hallelujah. So, I muster up some control, take a deep breath and I give a long drawn out flirty, "Maybeee. But I have a couple of questions for you."

"Shoot."

I fidget as my thoughts begin to run wild once again. What if he is a drug dealer, or a professional killer? Okay. Don't panic. Breathe. Deep breath. You don't know anything. Stop it!

"So." I say in an interrogation kind-of way.

"So." Ashton copies.

"Ok. I don't understand. I thought you were a bartender," I ask cautiously.

"No. I told you. I was a producer and an actor," he replies simply.

"But you were working as a bartender last night, right?" I ask.

"Yes. I was practicing last night for my latest movie role. The owners of the bar were kind enough to allow me to play a bartender last night as research and training for the role."

"Oh, come on. Just tell me the truth," I pause and shift uncomfortably. "Are you into something illegal? I mean—" I trail off.

"What? No! Don't you see? I don't pretend. I am just me. What you see is what you get. I know it's different." He watches as I give him a defensive cross-armed closed look. "Well, unless I'm acting. I often act as someone other than me, but I wasn't acting last night." Ashton says eloquently.

"Well, yes. I guess. It just seems a little unbelievable. It doesn't seem to add up." I ramble as I think through last night's events. Well, he did seem very real, but guys do that to impress girls. Right?

"I don't play emotional games. I gave that up years ago. I speak what's true for me," he says deliberately. "What do you mean by 'It doesn't add up'?"

"Well, you are what, thirty years old? This place must be worth ten million."

"Yes." He nods casually as if all thirty-year-olds have multi-million dollar homes.

"Well, how?" I ask.

"How?" He looks shocked that I asked him that.

"Yes. How are you making this kind of income?" I ask waiting for the lie to drop.

"Well, I get paid for the films I create." Ashton responds plainly.

I know what he's saying makes sense, but I'm not satisfied. I can't believe he's making millions. "And?" I probe. "I mean are you doing something illegal? You're not a drug dealer? Are you?"

"A drug dealer? Where did you get that?" Ashton asks innocently with a smile.

"I don't know. I'm trying to put the pieces together," I look down and sigh in frustration.

When I look up I find him looking at me with the purest, most peaceful face. I shake my head in regret. "I'm sorry. I'm being silly," I say starting to back-pedal as fast as possible.

His eyes find mine and he starts to laugh, "Look. I've worked hard and have been very involved in the film industry—both behind the scenes and in front of the camera. You may find this hard to believe, but some might call me a movie star," he says with an honest smile. "I've never even played a role as a criminal though," he laughs.

"Okay, I will believe you." I let it go and drop into a cross-legged seat on the floor as a laugh breaks through.

Ping. I reach for my phone across the floor. It's a text from Jake. I glance at it and turn my phone over as if it's nothing.

"It's okay." He sits behind me and wraps his arms and

legs around me. I'm not sure if he's responding to the text or my fight to make him wrong about making money, but I don't care.

I nod and smile, "Yeah. I guess so."

"Are you hungry?" he asks as he stands and reaches out a hand for me to do the same.

"Starved," I smile and take his hand.

"Okay. You should probably tell Jake something before he panics and thinks I kidnapped you. *Then* I might be considered a criminal." He giggles and nods to my phone. "You know, Rachael, I like you a lot, but I am not comfortable with dishonesty. If you are going to be with me today you need to tell him."

I find myself getting a protective armor, "So, what do you propose I tell him? That I met you last night and I am going horseback riding with you today? Oh and I may be out past dinner, because we may go out after?"

"That would be a start. Tell him the truth. You know they say the truth will set you free," he smiles.

"That's what I'm afraid of. He will set me free." I look up at Ashton with my best sad puppy eyes. "I'm not sure I want to be set free."

"It's okay. But if that's the case we'd better end this now. I'm not looking for a girl to share. I want to be with that adventurous, courageous, fun girl I met last night. The one that said she was a woman on a mission to change the world," Ashton says simply with no agenda.

"What are you really saying? Are you saying that I should say good-bye to my fiancé of two years after being with you for fifteen hours?" I'm starting to feel a little weak in my knees and my heart begins to race. Actually, the thought excites me, and it also scares the life out of me.

"I would like to see what's next for us," Ashton says directly to my heart.

"You would?" I reply feeling speechless. I don't know how to respond. A part of me feels as if I might be star struck, while another part is falling deeply in love with him. And now another part comes forth feeling terrified to end things with Jake.

"Why not? I feel deeply connected to you, and I trust that inner knowing. My being knows I love you, and that moves me to ask you to be with me. What I'm saying is every fiber of my being has been enveloped by this rich energy of joy when we're together," Ashton says straightly, "I can tell you feel it too—it's like making the earth move when were together. If things were going that well with Jake, you would have never gone out with me last night. Be open to the possibilities for us!" He makes this grand gesture with his hands and continues, "Rachael, you need to know, I am fine with whoever you choose, but you need to choose. I refuse to share and compromise."

I suddenly find myself wanting him to fight for me. I mean he says these amazing things, but he's still not asking me to choose him. I contemplate this for a minute as pictures start to infiltrate my mind. I see myself as the wife of this gorgeous movie star. I see romance, glamour, wealth and fame. A smile starts to breakthrough, and I look down avoiding his eyes. Then I ponder living a life with Jake, which isn't as beautiful, but it's secure, and I don't want to be alone. My eyes finally come up and meet his. "Umm—I don't know," I say biting my lower lip.

"Rachael, this is your choice. I have told you what I perceive for us. Now, what do *you* perceive for us?"

"I'm scared. What if it doesn't work out between us? What if you both chuck me? Where will I be then?"

Ashton's face is serene and he clearly says, "I live my life by following the energy flow. When something feels expansive—like it gives the energy room to grow—I know it's for me and I follow it. It feels true. When something feels confining—like it stifles the energy—I run like hell. It feels like a lie to me. I follow the flow by navigating the waves of energy." His eyes dart to mine to help me understand. "In other words, I simply follow what's feels like joy, bliss and ease and allow the universe to take me. We, through and as consciousness, create everything in our lives." He takes a deep breath, "Look, Rachael, you can continue to choose Jake. Your mind thinks he's your sure thing. But does that choice feel freeing or confining? Imagine following the energy in your world all the time and create something from that place," he smiles.

I peer at him. I know he means it. He is following his heart or energy as he says it. My body is shaking so hard it feels like a bowl of gelatin that has just been shaken. And the weird thing is that somewhere inside I do know. I have been denying it, but I do know what I have to do. And it totally sucks! It sucks because I'm going to hurt someone I really care about. I let out a long sigh and stare at the phone remorsefully.

2

Mixed Emotions

I AM IN WONDERLAND cruising down the California coast in Ashton's convertible after a beautiful horseback ride and fabulous meal. I'm still digesting the most remarkable homemade food from his friend Robert's house—Robert Downey, Jr. that is. Yep, I had dinner with Iron Man.

I'm not sure if it's the good food and fascinating people or Ashton that's causing this tingling tickle inside. For the first time in a really long time I feel alive. Maybe it's because we've spent most of the day laughing. And before the horseback riding adventure we found time to go shopping; I'm wearing these awesome DKNY jeans, a fun tee that Ashton chose for me, and some fabulous cowboy boots we found at a riding shop. All day our conversation topics have included relationships, sexual positions, and our wildest moments and deepest dreams. Nothing was off-limits.

When we turn into the front gate at Hollywood studios,

I have to admit it's not glamorous. I watch as Ashton points to various trailers telling me stories about Hollywood actors. As he rattles on I continue to nod, but don't really hear a word. My head just continues to sing, "Ashton, Ashton, Ashton." He loves me. Yummy, Ashton. Then suddenly my emotional high expands when the thought of being his girl drifts through my mind.

We park and walk down a long paved corridor lit by several large spotlights. I can tell Ashton's excited for me to be a part of his world—partly because he has suddenly become an animated speed-talking chipmunk. And partly because I can tell he's excited to show me the set for his film. I watch in bemusement.

He places the key in the studio door and as he goes to turn it, he looks me in the eyes and whispers, "Ready?"

"Yes, of course." I respond quietly with a hint of giddiness.

In one sweeping motion, Ashton opens the studio door and turns on all the lights including little ones illuminating a beautiful, hand-crafted Eiffel tower.

"Wow," I respond, my jaw dropped open in awe.

He looks at me and smiles. "What do you think? Do you like it? It's cool, eh?"

"Yes! It's gorgeous. It looks like the real thing. I mean, I've never seen the real thing, but this is what I'd imagine it looks like," I say in amazement.

"I knew you'd like it," he laughs. "Come on." He tugs my right arm, and together we fall into a full run across the studio. My boots create a loud echo throughout the room.

When we come to a stop he turns to me and places his forefinger over his lips and whispers, "Shhhh—Listen."

I stand still with anticipation as he turns a knob and presses a button on the wall. Suddenly, the room fills with French music. It sounds like the crescendo at the final moment in a romantic film. Ashton grabs my hands and starts dancing with me.

"Whoa. Wow." I respond slowly with awe. I know I sound like a parrot that only knows the word "wow," but I don't care.

Ashton smiles and looks deeply into my eyes. "I love you, Rachael," he says with unique authenticity.

"I think I love you too," I reply back.

"You think?" he responds.

The music changes. He takes my right hand and gives me a little twirl and dip to the music. I laugh hysterically at his surprising, playful nature. Who is this guy? He's truly phenomenal, I think for the hundredth time, which unfortunately also comes with this inner whisper that says too bad I'm not good enough for him.

"Yes, I think I really do in fact love you. I do," I say purposely teasing him.

His mouth twitches slightly, and then like a sneaky villain he says, "Hey, I have a surprise for you."

"There's more?" I ask.

"Of course, there's more. There's always more. You haven't seen anything yet." He sweeps me up in his arms and begins stepping up to the Eiffel tower landing. It looks just like the top of the tower, but is only one flight of stairs up.

When we arrive at the top he slowly drops me to my feet and gives me a mischievous grin.

"What? What are you up to?" I ask nervously biting my pinky fingernail.

"Look up," Ashton points for me to look up at the dark planetarium sky on the studio ceiling.

"Um, wow," My jaw drops in awe.

As our eyes become glued to the starry sky, he pulls me closer and I snuggle with him, placing my arm around his waist and sneaking it inside his shirt. For a moment we stand there completely connected with tingles running through my body. Then the sky—I mean ceiling—lights up with twinkles, and I feel all lit up. I gaze at the firework display in the fake starry sky. I hold my breath waiting for the next big burst. I've never seen anything so magical.

"You don't do anything small, do you?" I joyously ask.

He smiles. "Not usually. I came to play big," he responds and drops to one knee.

I look down at him speechlessly and start shaking my head in disbelief. I see his right hand tightly squeezed around this small box. My heart is pounding. My palms are sweating. I don't believe it. It can't be. Of course it's not a ring. It's only been twenty-four hours since we first met, but it doesn't stop my pounding heart.

His eyes meet mine with a serious look. My head starts shaking in denial. It's probably earrings or a pendant. I'm sure it's nothing. Of course it's nothing.

He looks me directly in the eyes, opens the box and says, "Will you?"

I drop my head back laughing hysterically. It's two tickets to see Madonna in concert next weekend. "Yes! Yes! Yes!" I leap into his arms with a tight hug.

After our studio adventure, Ashton takes me to his favorite sidewalk café for a late-night treat. The waiter delivers our strawberry milkshake with two straws. Ashton's rambling on about how the café is family-owned and the only thing that really keeps it in business is—but before I can hear the rest I gasp. I see Jake approaching us. Am I hallucinating? I glance again through my hair. Damn, I'm one hundred percent sure it's him. I lean to Ashton and whisper, "I need a new straw; this one has an air leak," and I squat to hide under the side of the table.

"Sorry? What are you doing?" Ashton asks.

"Nothing. I'll be right back," I say as I crawl to the side of the café to seek refuge. Shit. What is Jake doing here? Did someone tip him off? I curiously peek around the corner. OMG. Ashton and Jake are now talking. Oh no. Now, they are hugging with that three-guy-back-pat hug thing they do. What? What the hell? Oh no, I think Jake just spotted me. I duck back behind the side of the building.

A few moments later I peek around again and Jake's gone. Wow. That was close. I straighten up, collect myself and walk to our table with trembling hands and a weak heart.

"Who was that?" I innocently ask Ashton as I plop back in my chair.

"Where's your straw?" Ashton asks focusing on my hands with the missing straw.

"Um, they were out. Who was that?" I ask again hoping to hear the back story about his relationship with Jake.

"Oh. That was my good friend Jake, from college. He is great. I haven't seen him in years!" He says with enthusiasm. He takes a swallow of the milkshake. Ashton is completely sparkling with true joy at the thought of seeing his long lost friend. Lovely, Ashton is friends with my ex-fiancé Jake. What are the chances? This just can't be a good sign.

"That's fantastic. Too bad he couldn't stay," I say with an unauthentic tone of dismay.

"He's meeting his date down the street," he smiles. "Actually, it was really nice to see him again. We used to hang out all the time, but our lives and careers went in very different directions."

"Really?" I respond in a fake tone. My head is stuck on Jake going out on a date. We just broke up. The only person who lives close to here is Katie. Could Jake be dating Katie? Has he been cheating on me? I'm firing up inside with anger at the thought.

"Are you okay?" Ashton interrupts my thoughts.

I let out a deep sigh, "Um. I was just thinking. I mean, it just occurred to me," I stall, waiting for something good to come to mind. I feel for a moment that I need to come clean about Jake, but instead I say, "Where did you go to school?" I smile straightening up, slightly proud of my little diversion.

"UCLA. I didn't give college a try until a few years after high school though, and only went for a year. When I got the lead role in *New Lord* I dropped out and have been in the film business ever since. Acting was love at first sight," he says as his face lights up.

I nod and give him a look that says, "you want to kiss me because I'm so cute."

Ashton gazes at me for a few moments, "So, do you want to get out of here?"

"Yes," I say feeling a flush creep over my face.

On the drive back to his place my thoughts are still lamenting the loss of Jake. I know it was my decision to move on, but how could he have moved on so fast? I can't believe this.

We park, and as I reach for the car door handle Ashton whispers, "Stop. Wait."

"Okay," I stop.

"You are a million miles away. Where are you? Where did you go?" I watch as he reaches into the center console and takes something out. And that something is now in his jacket pocket.

"I have a few thoughts running through my mind. I'm sorry," I squeak, finding my noisy mind quieting again.

"Would you be willing to collect all those scattered pieces of you and come back here, because I have something I want to ask you?" He smiles.

I turn and look to him with slight confusion, "Yes. I can do that," I say feeling a little spark of curiosity inside.

He steps out of the car and runs to my door. "Can I show you something?" He smiles like a giddy little school boy.

"Of course." We walk slowly with fingers interlaced. My body is shaking with anticipation.

"Are you cold?" Ashton asks opening the front door of his house.

I don't respond. I'm not cold, but I'm shivering with an overwhelming sense of excitement.

Now that I'm here with Ashton my thoughts about Jake have subsided. Thoughts of gentle, soft, tender kisses enter my body. I imagine our sweet embrace. I imagine the sensuousness, the caress and caring. This starts a sensation in my body that is way beyond words.

"Rachael, I totally, utterly, completely adore you," Ashton says with words, and I can tell his body feels this energetic sensuality I feel in mine. "Have a seat," he gestures to the sofa.

Then in a single heartbeat he kneels down in front of me and says, "Rachael, I totally adore you and I would love if you would do me the pleasure of sharing your life with me." And with that he pulls out a diamond ring and says, "Will you?"

3

Something New

I WAKE TO A SHUFFLE under the sheets. I start my regular orientation and questioning process. Where am I? What happened? What grand adventures will happen today? I keep my eyes closed until I find my thoughts coming in clearly—they sound something like oh my goodness, wow, I can't believe this, I am dreaming.

I roll on my belly and stretch out my left arm and gaze at my left ring finger. It's true. It's true, Ashton asked me to be his partner in life. And I said yes. I'm engaged!

Last night we laughed, talked, cuddled and connected in a way I never knew possible. I gaze over at Ashton still half asleep. I giggle slightly.

"Hi love," he says in a groggy tone.

"Hi." I feel like I've known him all my life—many, many lifetimes, actually. I'm so in love. And I'm so grateful we found each other.

I couldn't wait to share the news with Katie. I left her a

message yesterday, but I haven't received a response. In her defense, I called around midnight and it's now just seven this morning. I don't know why, but I'm afraid she and Jake had an "evening" as well. Yesterday it really mattered, but now, I don't care. I'm engaged to a movie star! That's all that matters right now.

Suddenly I see Ashton give an almighty stretch. He lets out a big yawn. He's so cute.

"Good morning, love. Come here," he grabs me and I cuddle placing my cheek on his hairy chest.

"Good morning," I sing in response.

"Hey, I was thinking. Do you want to go to Vegas?" he asks.

"Um. I guess. Someday. But first let's enjoy some coffee." I reply thinking I need to get back to my life. I mean, it's been an exciting weekend, but now that it's Monday, I should probably get my butt back to work. I'm the receptionist at a shoe repair shop. It's not the best job, but I am learning more about shoes so I'm fine with it.

"Why wait? I don't start my next film for another two weeks. Let's play until then. Whatcha say? Wouldn't it be fun for us?"

"Of course! I've never been to Vegas. Jake and I discussed it once, but it just never worked out with his busy schedule," I catch myself saying Jake's name. I don't want Ashton to ask too many questions about him. I'm sure it's not good for our relationship if he knew he stole his good friend's girlfriend—especially after my little escape last night at the café.

"Sweet! Well, I'm happy to be your first. A Vegas virgin.

I love it!" he says with a big evil grin and a Dr. Evil hand gesture. "Can you get time off work? Can we go today? What will it take?"

"Um. Yes. I'll make some calls and see what I have to do," I say feeling a little uncomfortably excited with his spontaneity. I guess I better get used to it. I mean, I may actually go through that marriage step this time.

"Cool. Want to join me in the shower my Vegas virgin?" he asks cutely changing the subject.

"Um. Sure. But, you know, I want to wait." I smile and nod expecting him to know what I mean when I make a little finger circling gesture.

"Yes. I know. We'll clean our bodies. The shower is big enough for two." His words trail off sarcastically.

"Okay," I reply dropping my head back and we both peel into laughter.

Later that day, we arrive at the Las Vegas Paris Hotel. We've had an amazing drive and talked about everything under the sun. I knew it would be an amazing trip when Ashton started by asking, "If you could be and do anything in this world what would it be? What really moves you?"

Off I went to sharing my dreams and fantasies about being the founder of an inspirational designer shoe label and how every shoe would give back to the greater good in some way. Then he asked me about joy and what joy meant to me. Finally, we got into this crazy "woo-woo weird" conversation which started with him saying, "I walk on the earth but I'm not from it. I know that I've lived many lives on this planet and others. Do you ever feel that way?"

"I guess. I've never quite thought about it that way. I don't have a memory of it, but something inside me says it could be a possibility," I had replied feeling a little awkward.

"What if you didn't have to remember? What if you just knew?" he asked.

"What do you mean by that?"

"Do you remember when I talked about following the energies that are expanding? When something feels light and joyful inside it's like a street arrow to follow. In other words, that is the way of least resistance. It's like flowing downstream in a river instead of swimming against the current."

"Um. Yes. I see." I pause. "I've never really thought about it that way."

"This is my way of life. It allows my life to have great simplicity, and it allows me to know that I'm on the right path," he laughs, "which is awesome. It allows me to trust consciousness and instinct. Cool?" Ashton smiles and grabs my hand.

"Cool. Then yes. It does feel true that I would have had many lives, maybe on many different planets." I laughed, "I guess I can trust my consciousness and instinct too."

We continued talking about life growing up, our parents, and our favorite hobbies. I told Ashton about my parents and their life-ending car accident when I was sixteen. He told me about his adventure-filled life with his family. He shared his most intimate and grand life experiences. I have to admit, it's a little intimidating when you're with a man who spends his time bareback horse-riding and cliff-jumping in Mexico, while you spend yours going to bars and watching movies.

When we arrive in Vegas, I feel as if I'm in someone's imagination. The air on the Vegas strip is filled with changs, cha-chings and cheers. The smell of money is on the street. It's as if an entire city is having a party.

"Ready for some fun?" Ashton asks with his cute animated gestures.

"Of course," I reply while mocking his arm gestures.

"Come on silly girl," he says interlacing his fingers in mine.

We drive through the front entrance of the Las Vegas Paris Hotel and allow a valet to take the car. We check in, drop off our bags in our suite, and after an intimate moment and elevator ride we are down at the nearest casino. "What's your flava?" He laughs as he drops a quarter in the slot machine and places my hand on the lever, "Give it a whirl."

"What? Flava?" I pull the lever and feel as if I've been transported into cha-ching wonderland.

"What do you want to do? Craps? Blackjack? Slots? What's your flava?" asks Ashton.

"I'm game. Let's just play. You take the lead," I say with a little spin after pulling the next slot machine's lever.

"Not bad. You just added five bucks to the money making pile. How much more can we add to that tonight?"

Finally, after a few hours of serious playing, we wander past a small chapel into a French café.

We sit and order two croissants and black coffees, and by the time our food arrives Ashton and I are in full conversation about getting married in Vegas. We talk about a dress, inviting his parents, and even the bouquet. He jokes and says it's just one choice away.

I look at him and realize that he is totally serious. Funny how I think we are having a joking hypothetical conversation and he's ready to take action. Finally, I say, "No. You are insane. We aren't ready. We don't know each other well enough."

"Well, let's put it to the test. Okay? You can say no if you'd like," he teases. "Truth. Do you desire to spend your life with me?" he asks in a real, honest tone.

"Yes." I nod.

"Does that path allow your energy to expand? Does your instinct say yes?" he asks.

"Yes." I nod.

"Here's the thing. There is no time. Time is a construct that we create in this reality. Now is the only time we have. The past is a mere memory and the future is all fantasy. So when I say these weird things like 'let's get married,' I don't really look at it on a time continuum. I live now." He looks at me and waits to make sure I get it.

I sit there for a moment processing what he just said. I feel somewhat manipulated to buy into it, and at the same time my heart feels one hundred percent in, and time would change that. I finally say, "I like it," and nod several times playfully. "The only thing stopping me is my fear. My fear that when you really know who I am you won't like me," I say, pushing out my lower lip.

"What? Who are you pretending to be?" Ashton asks curiously.

"Um. Yeah. I'm not sure," I shrug.

"Well, let's see. Are you trying to be someone that you think I want you to be? Someone you think you should be to be with me? Someone you think you'll become? Someone you decided you'll become? Or someone you defined yourself as?" Ashton stops and waits for a reply.

"Yes. All that I think. Ugh." I roll my eyes.

"I know. And you know what?" Ashton asks.

"What?"

"I also know who you are underneath all that," Ashton replies.

"You do?"

"Yes. I do." It's so sweet how he pronounces, "I do."

"I do too." I say seriously about myself and the upcoming nuptials.

Ashton laughs. "Silly girl. Finish your croissant and we can get your dress, flowers, garter and whatever else your heart desires."

"Really?" I say as I bite my lip and push the plate to the side. "Finished."

Of course our first stop is the elegant shoe store across the corridor. My emotions are running in cycles from terror to ecstatic joy. As we browse the beautiful selection, I start talking about shoe manufacturing and the history of shoes. And once again I ramble on about my dream to own a conscious-based shoe label.

He joyously listens and watches me in delight as I try on no less than fifty pairs of designer heels. Finally when it looks like I've narrowed it down to two pairs he says, "So what's the verdict? Who wins? Prada or Louboutin?"

I look joyously at both pairs. "Hmmm," I say waiting for one shoe to scream louder than the other.

"If you are serious about getting married tomorrow, we may need to get a dress and a few other things done. So, whatcha think?" he says with a wink urging me to decide.

"Here's the thing. Shoes are very important." I state rather grandly. "In fact, it's probably the most important thing. You see, I believe your shoes are the gateway to infinite intelligence. They have to move you. I choose this one. This one moves me." With the biggest smile I hold up the Louboutins. "Christian Louboutin falls in my top five footwear designers. Let's honor him and my infinite being today!" I say with a little smirk.

"I say those definitely move me from my infinite. They've got *sole*!" Ashton teases and gives me a dancer's twirl in the three inch heels. "Are you ready to look for your dress, flowers, and arrange a chapel?"

Two hours later we have almost everything: a tuxedo, a dress, slippers, a chapel, a bouquet of sterling roses, and a blue garter. I share the list with Ashton, "Okay, there's just one thing missing. We have something new, something blue, something borrowed—we need something old."

He looks at me and asks, "What's the significance of having all those items checked off your list?"

I stare at him for a minute. "Well, obviously I don't want to jinx things from the start. And I don't want to have it looming over my head that things didn't work out because I didn't have something old. I know it's silly, but humor me."

"Do you really believe in karma?" he asks curiously.

"Well—no—but I don't want to take any chances either," I say with a silly smile.

"You're too cute. So, you do believe in karma. Okay. Let's get you something old then." The next thing I know he stops a woman on the strip who's wearing a beautifully-jeweled antique barrette in her hair. She had her reservations about parting with it, but after a brief conversation Ashton and the woman finally agree, and she's ecstatic to receive the thousand dollars for it. He hands me the barrette and says, "Don't make it significant."

"Why?" I ask.

"As soon as you make anything significant you create judgment and separation," he replies.

"But it is important." I argue, admiring the barrette.

"Well, that's the conclusion you've made, but it is just a barrette."

"It's an old barrette," I reply. "Oh. Yes it is," I tease. "So, does that mean that I will never be your significant other?" I say jokingly.

"Exactly," he replies honestly.

"Oh," I say in dismay.

"Here's the thing. We live each moment in choice. What if each day we could choose to be together all over again? What if we didn't have to define our relationship based on the construct of time and over time? This way we can infinitely love and choose to be together in every moment," he says rather grandly.

I smile, but I have to admit I'm not sure how I feel about that. I understand this idea of choice and free will, but I would like to feel there is something more between us than how he feels in each moment. "So, does that mean if in two hours you don't like me, we won't go through with this?"

"What? No. This is about truly choosing each other instead of having to be together."

"So, any idea how long you'll choose me? A lifetime? More than a lifetime?" I ask.

"Well, it seems as if I keep choosing you lifetime after lifetime, so I would probably say yes, definitely a lifetime," he smiles.

Feeling satisfied, I reply back with a nod.

With an assortment of shopping bags in hand, we walk into the chapel and ask the receptionist for dates and times as to when we can arrange our wedding.

She runs her hand down a page, and screws up her mouth. Finally she light-heartedly responds, "How about tomorrow at two?"

We both look at each other and nod in unison. "Perfect," replies Ashton.

"Fab. I'll put you down," she says with a mouthful of gum.

4

My Five Year Coma

I HEAR A VOICE from the television, "Studio Hollywood spotlight on Brock's Blissful Soles."

"Wait!" I yell to the television as I dash to see him.

"I love this man's shoe line. I own six fabulous pairs." I say enthusiastically to Silvia, our housekeeper. "I believe shoes offer insights into our souls. And his sandals scream to me: Rachael you are beautiful, poised and potent just as you are. You go girl!" I smile at Silvia, who is now chopping onions, "What do you think?"

She looks up at me with tearful eyes and nods, but her face isn't convincing.

For the past five years, I have made it my priority to meet nearly every famous designer in the world. Unfortunately, I have never been honored to meet the amazing Pierre Brock. Pierre lives a simple, low-profile and somewhat anti-social life. This lifestyle is fabulous for him, but doesn't allow many opportunities to be in his presence.

The Studio Hollywood show continues, "Thousands of women are now embracing a new inspiration. Blissful Soles are causing the women of Hollywood and around the global to drool over these hard-to-not-love sandals. Brock says they were inspired by his twin princesses, Lucy and Gaby." I see a sudden flash of his twin daughters. The image fades to the host, who says, "We leave you tonight with a clip from Ashton Hunt's newest film, which reminds us to connect with our inner knowing, *The Revelation*." Silvia rushes over to see it, and I let out a frustrated sigh.

"No! Wait! Show me Pierre! I can see Ashton anytime," I whine to the television.

Today is the big release of Ashton's newest film. The truth is, I am just plain sick of hearing about it. My mind right now would rather indulge in Pierre Brock's Blissful Soles journey than Ashton's newest flick. Ashton has talked, talked, and talked about it for the last few months, and my mind is so tired of hearing about how it will change how people see this world. Ugh. And the biggest problem is, when he's not talking about it he's just too much. He's so present with food, sex, play and life that he's too much to take. I used to love those things about him, but lately all these intense sensations are just overwhelming. Honesty, I'm glad the film is done. Done. Done. Done. I will finally have my Ashton back. Maybe things will feel right again then. I can see it now. We'll take our private jet and fly off to Martha's Vineyard. There we will enjoy days of spa treatments, intense shoe shopping and vineyard trips on horseback. This is how we used to be together and play. I reminisce about the fun we had from our last few trips. I remember feeling like all we needed and wanted to focus on was each other. It seems like it's been a long time, but our last trip was just four months ago when we visited Napa Valley.

Suddenly, my phone shrills and I am jolted back to the present moment. Where is it? C'mon. I know it's here somewhere. I toss a few couch pillows aside and I grab it. It's Ashton.

"Hey baby," I say in my everyday monotone voice, as if I am completely unaware they are showing his trailer on many entertainment shows right now. I love Ashton, but I'm not so keen on his Hollywood movie career. And I'm definitely not keen on being his Hollywood trophy wife—his "yummy wifey" as he puts it. I see Hollywood as a big castle and once you are in, you are in. And once you're in you have to follow the rules or all the evils dragons in the moat will eat you. If you don't show up with a fit body, designer clothes and a beautiful smile on your face, you're dead. And if you break a rule, whatever rule you broke will be spread worldwide through the media. I used to have these big ideas about being a famous shoe designer, but now I spend my time looking the part of Ashton's trophy wife.

"Hey sweetness, guess what?" He's bursting with excitement. "Oh, you'll never guess. I just sent you the VIP Platinum Pass to the studio for my going away party." He pauses and his tone changes, "Darling, there's been a little change of plans for the next film project—I'm leaving tonight instead of Monday." He can tell that I am angry with the change of plans. This isn't the first time. "Baby, I'm sorry. I just found out, but it's for the better. You know how these guys are. We have to leave early so we can meet with some big time hot shots in Paris." He pauses and waits for me to speak. When I don't, he says, "It's just a couple of days."

"Ashton!" My voice becomes a high-pitch shrill. "How could you?" Anger is brewing to the point it's creating hot steam inside me. "I feel like you are in love with orgasmic food, sex, and your job—and not me. I mean it used to be all about me. What happened?" The words just come rushing out without warning.

"Rach. Come on. You know how it is. I live presently. This is a part of living for me. You are a part of living for me. I love you—I can't just be with you right now," he trails off in a loving tone.

"I know. It's fine," I lie.

The truth is Ashton and I hardly ever fight. Except maybe the incident when I came home with Bella, our new little golden retriever puppy. I have known since the day we were married that Ashton didn't want children. I didn't know this included an adorable puppy. But that doesn't count because Ashton even admitted that he completely overreacted. Now that I think about it, perhaps we have had the odd dispute about Bella. Actually I think that's all we argue about. Who's feeding, walking and brushing her— perhaps Ashton on occasion has asked in exasperation, "Are you ever going to take this dog for a walk or are you going to let her pee in the house?" And perhaps we have had the odd, frank discussion about how many hours Ashton works. He loves his work as an actor, and maybe just a few times I have accused him of loving his work more than me. The point is, we are a great couple. We recently agreed that Ashton would stop complaining about Bella and I would stop whining about his work. And then Ashton went back to the studio and I went to Whole Foods and returned home to a dog covered in down feathers from our bed pillows. The point is, we always work it out.

"Ashton," I whine, "I don't want to go to another work party where we pretend to be something we're not."

"What?" he curiously and innocently asks. After five years of marriage I can honestly say Ashton never has any expectations about how we have to show up together, which makes me think he honestly has no idea what I'm talking about. "What do you mean pretending? This is our life, not a movie. Just come as you."

"Never mind. It's fine," I reply with a fake smile big enough for him to hear.

"Are you sure? Do you want to talk about this?" he genuinely asks.

"No. I'm being silly. I'll see you tonight," I reply putting on my happy tone—noticing once again that I'm excellent at playing the role of the happy wife.

"Okay," he replies and pauses. Then with a joyful tone he says, "Hey. Did you see the clip on Studio Hollywood? What did you think?" He sounds like a child that just had his first gumball.

"I didn't see it. You called right when they were playing it," I respond vaguely.

"No worries. Hey, I'll see you tonight. I want you here by my side before I leave. Lots of hugs and kisses from me until I see you! Mwah!" He always does that. His excitement is so endearing that it's impossible to stay angry at him. And to be honest, I find him so cute when he rambles on with delight.

The last time Ashton had a studio party, I showed up three hours late to prove my independence, and in that short time some major media blog had announced me as a no show. The headlines read, "Where's Rachael Hunt? She's MIA at Ashton Hunt's Premiere." I had completely intended on going, I was just proving that I had a choice in the matter. Really.

So I say what I always say, "Okay. I will see you there. Meet me at the gate in fifteen minutes." I hypnotically click off the phone, drop it on the table and mindlessly strip down as I wander into my closet to find something to wear. There's a brand new white Tahari linen dress lying on the floor of my closet. I wore it for the first time two nights ago when Ashton flew us out to our new villa in the country. I pick it up and survey it as a possibility. The rule in Hollywood is to never get caught wearing the same outfit twice. I guess this will work, being that only Ashton has seen it and no photos were taken.

The dress is a size two and slightly too small, but I didn't want to indulge size four. It is forbidden in this crazy Hollywood world. I slip the dress over my head and stare at myself in the full length bedroom mirror in dismay.

As I fix the back zipper on the dress, I think back through

our years of marriage. Ashton has spent years getting me to choose for me and it's completely impossible—especially in Hollywood. Shall I count the ways?

1. I am obligated to show up as Ashton's yummy wifey. This is the role I play most of the time. Sometimes I feel I'm a better actor than he is.

2. I starve myself most of the time so I can fit in with the Hollywood quota—a size two. Then I still have to suck in my stomach all night and pretend to be thinner than I am. Not to mention that I always feel wrong when I want to eat just the smallest carbohydrate—especially by myself.

3. I pretend to have intelligent conversations about films including the costumes, lights, sounds and script. I'm like a broken record and in constant alignment and agreement with Ashton's fellow cast members. I should just bring a recording that says "Oh my! Yes! That was incredible!" when you press play.

As I sloppily slap on some eyeliner and touch up my make-up I find myself staring back at me and asking, What's wrong with me? Why do I feel this way? I know I should be incredibly grateful for what we have—shouldn't I? I drop the blush brush and support myself with both hands, looking in the bathroom mirror as I will myself not to cry. No, it's fine. It'll be fine. Come on, Rachael, you are better than this. And with that I give myself a strong look down my body to my feet. As I see my bare toes, I think about my heel options for the evening. And out of the blue an image of Pierre from Studio Hollywood spotlight drifts through my mind and I choose my Blissful Soles. I slip on the left foot and it yells,

"Rachael, you are a poised and potent woman!" and as I place the right one I hear, "Rachael, you are phenomenal!" which releases a big smile across my face. I do feel poised and potent. Yes. I CAN do this.

Exactly fifteen minutes later I arrive at *The Revelation* studio party. I try not to get too emotional when I discover rain rapidly falling on my brand-new Italian red leather jacket, which I am now using as a makeshift umbrella. Now rain is blowing into my face as I run to the front gate where I meet Ashton to gain entrance into the party. At a moment like this, Ashton would say something like, What's the joy in this? Unfortunately, at this moment I can't muster such a light thought.

When I finally reach Ashton, he greets me with an enormous umbrella and the warmest hug, and for a beautiful moment everything is glorious. I'm not exactly sure how he can take all this pain away, but I'm grateful when it happens. As we embrace I feel a tingle spread through my body, and I notice how awesome he looks tonight in his six piece custom-designed suit and his snazzy snakeskin boots. I love him so much—I just wish he could be like other guys and keep me out of his workplace. He dips me as if we were dancing, and I wonder if it's a show for his fellow actor friends, but there is no one around. We embrace with a kiss when without warning a car crazily speeds by splashing through a huge puddle and drenching us with a muddy waterfall. The water pours over us and I slip backward. Luckily, Ashton swoops down like my knight in shining armor, and for a moment I find my footing. Then with a step forward, I end up on my back with Ashton on top of me laughing hysterically as if it's some big joke. We try to get up and we both slip again, Ashton thinks it's funny, but I can't even muster up anything except anger. I'm pissed. Finally, I sit up and start to assess the damage to my shoes and coat. I remorsefully take off my ruined shoes when a golf cart arrives splashing a little more mud onto my legs—you have to be kidding me!

"Wow, what a mess! Let me take you to wardrobe so you can get cleaned up," the cart driver says from beneath her layers of rain gear. "I'll have someone meet you there." She murmurs some instructions into her CB radio as we get settled in the cart. I can feel the mud soaking into my underwear.

"I'm sure you'll be able to find plenty to change into in wardrobe. It'll be fine," Ashton says with deep compassion.

"Whatever." I flippantly reply knowing that going home and hiding under the covers is preferred, but not an option.

When the cart stops at the women's backstage wardrobe, Ashton gives me a warm look, "Hey, text me when you're ready, and I'll meet you."

"Okay," I respond, thinking that he wants to get me by his side as soon as possible to avoid any celebrity gossip.

I open the wardrobe door and I'm greeted by a familiar-looking twenty-something girl with an enthusiastic smile. "Wow," she looks at me with a mix of awe and pity, "looks like you didn't quite escape the weather. We have plenty of great pieces to choose from on the racks there." She gestures to rows of clothing behind her.

Feeling annoyed and rebellious, I head to the casual-looking selections. I choose a modern pair of bell bottom jeans and a ZZ Top tee shirt from the rack. It's cool, hip, but not exactly party-appropriate. Oh well, I think with a little evil laugh. I look at myself in the full-length mirror and start to put on some fabulous seventies hoop earrings. Wow. I really don't give a shit anymore; tears fall down my cheek.

"Are you okay?" the girl asks. I know she can tell I'm not emotionally stable "We have dresses too," she adds innocently.

"No. Really, I'm fine," I say securing the left earring.

She thrusts out her right hand in front of my chest and enthusiastically says, "I'm Lucy. I'm so excited to meet you. I'm a huge fan."

"Of mine?" I shake her hand in disbelief. Trying to place where I have seen her.

She takes a quick breath and rapidly continues, "Rachael Hunt—wow," she says almost as if it's one word. "Wow. You're a pretty big deal. I mean, um, you're Ashton's wife, right? How exciting! I can only imagine the life you must lead. The parties, the clothes, the cars, the lifestyle— it's impressive. You are sooo lucky." She looks down at her hands and then says, "I'm just a receptionist. I mean I'm an aspiring make-up artist, but right now I work at one of Brock's boutiques. Brock is one of the shoe suppliers for *The Revelation*. Oh, I'm sorry I'm going on and on with my whining." She takes a quick breath, "I'll help you find a new pair of shoes to wear. My life isn't very exciting, huh? So, what's it like?" She rambles in bizarre directions while I try to remember where I've seen her.

"Excuse me?" I stare at her dumbfounded. I have not heard a word she has said. My head got stuck on "Brock" and "shoes," and now I'm fantasizing about Pierre Brock and his beautiful and blissful shoes. Did she just say Pierre Brock is a supplier for the film? I can't get my head around this. I wonder why Ashton didn't tell me—he knows how much Brock's shoe line means to me. Augh, I'll get him for that one.

"Oh, Gawd. I'm sorry. I just got excited. Wow. Ashton," she rambles. I'm not one hundred percent sure she's even speaking English. "I've obviously had too much coffee. I'm sorry; I know I have rambled on. I'm sorry to bother you. Would you like me to help you find some new shoes? I love that style." She takes another very brief breath. "Wow, you're a legend around here." I follow her towards a large rack of display shoes, when she says, "But, what I don't understand is why you wish for something else? I know you wish things were different. Do you wish things were different?" she says all in one breath as she pulls a heel from the shoe box.

I gasp, "Wow. They're beautiful." It's a stiletto with a sixties rainbow strap across the ankle and toes. "Wait," I pull my foot back and take a breath. "Lucy." I wait for a second to compose my words, "How long has Pierre been a part of this project?" I probe.

"Oh. You know. Since the film selected him as the footwear provider. Something like that." She pauses; I can tell she's anxiously waiting for me to respond to her earlier question about my life.

Dang. Ashton would have known Pierre was the

supplier. Why didn't he tell me? "Is Mr. Brock here?" I ask as I fasten the shoe strap and my heart starts to race at the thought of meeting him.

"Oh. No. He's a creator of shoes. He's not big on parties," she says, "I'm here to represent the brand."

"Got it," I nod in dismay allowing a single tear to roll down my cheek.

"Oh. You'll meet him one day," she nods sympathetically.

"It's not that, but the answer to your question is yes. Yes, I wish things were different." I start telling her about all the annoying things I deal with because I'm married to a movie actor and producer. I tell her how I've lost sight of who I really am. How I trail around after Ashton day in and day out showing the world that we have this glorious life that I'm not even sure I'm a part of.

We're interrupted by a knock on the door. A server stops in with a Manhattan. "For Mrs. Hunt" she says quickly. Ashton must have had it sent to me in efforts to calm my nerves. Here he is being so thoughtful while I'm completely losing it. I barely take a sip of the drink before my phone beeps with a text message. I stare at it for a second. It's from Ashton. **Hey sweetness r u ready?**

"What is it?" Lucy curiously asks. I'm not sure if she is referring to my rant or the text. "Lucy, I have to go. Please don't tell anyone, you know, what I told you tonight. It could really be damaging to Ashton's career."

She nods compassionately, "Yes. I promise."

"Ashton is leaving for a long trip tonight. I have to be with him," I tell her as I give my outfit one last look.

"Oh, I know. They've been planning this night for weeks." Lucy replies quickly and follows it by placing her hand over her mouth as if she has misspoken.

"What? He told me it was sprung on him tonight," I say exasperated, hoping Lucy will tell me more.

She shrugs, "Oh, you know, I'm wrong. You're right. They probably just sprung it on him tonight." She pauses innocently. "Wow. You look fabulous by the way. You are glowing. And you look very hip," she winks.

"I guess." I enthusiastically display my fabulous shoes. Now, I'm once again faking my positive outlook. I feel as if my marriage has plunged into a very dark place. Ashton is now keeping secrets. Secrets about his trip, about Pierre, and who knows what else. I hear another text ping: **love - where are u?**

I type: **still in wardrobe, OK!** and press send angrily.

A couple of seconds later, he replies: **darlin... im outside, u okay? We need to leave soon**

I stand up finding my thoughts running a million miles in a circle. Soon? I haven't been in wardrobe changing for that long. Geesh. I turn and look for Lucy to give her a big sisterly hug but she has disappeared. Oh well. I take a deep breath and emerge confidently from the room.

"Ta da!" I take his right hand and force a twirl as if nothing is wrong.

"Oh. Seventies style. Cool." He smiles, "You look great." He opens his arms and embraces me. Tears begin to well up in my eyes once again as sadness and anger come over me. I feel like a big emotional boulder is crushing down on me. Our marriage is crashing with dirty secrets and lies, and now he's leaving.

After making the necessary appearances at the party it's time for Ashton to begin the long night of travel. "Will you walk with me towards the helicopter landing?" he asks.

I nod.

Before we start walking he looks deeply into my tear-filled eyes and with an excitement in his voice he says, "Hey, come with me. It'll be five weeks of greatness. I can have Silvia take care of the dog. You'll love Fiji. I can see it now. We wake up each morning to an ocean breeze and the rising sun creating a beautiful sweep across the new horizon. We'll be watching from our warm, posh, featherbed. And then I'll surround your body with my warmth and we'll relish in the gratitude of the new day ahead because we both know a new Fiji adventure awaits—whether it's snorkeling, horseback riding or shopping." He smiles, "So, what do you think? Will you join me?"

Ashton has a way of making everything sound visually delicious, but in reality it is just not that beautiful. Actually, it might be for him. This is how he sees and lives life. This is one of the many traits that attracted me to him. When he asked me to marry him, he verbally painted a gorgeous picture of us traveling, dancing and making love. However, there wasn't anything in there about him going to Fiji to make a movie and leaving me alone on the beach or at home for weeks.

"Ashton, I know how these films go. You are on the set twelve to fourteen hours straight and then every night you prepare for the next day and read through your scripts. You won't be there with me and I'll be alone experiencing Fiji."

We walk out the back entrance towards the helicopter landing. Once we are clear of eavesdropping fans Ashton continues his plea. "Rachael, it doesn't have to be that way. We create our lives. Let's create a beautiful picture together in Fiji. Please come," he asks, but he knows I have already made my decision.

When we reach the landing, a bald man pops out from the helicopter and says, "Ashton, we have to leave now. We don't want to run into any weather." The man looks mildly agitated with my presence. In fact, he seems downright annoyed when he hears that Ashton has invited me to come along.

"Is he okay?" I ask Ashton.

"Oh, he's always that way," Ashton sighs.

"Ashton, are you sure about this trip?" I ask in dismay. "Something inside me doesn't feel right. Please don't go."

"Maybe what doesn't feel right is that we won't be together. Rachael, please come. You can shop in Paris along the way. There are designer boutiques all over the city. I'm sure I can make arrangements." He starts nodding hoping I'll join in. "Look, I've already packed a couple of Vuitton bags for you. So, what do you say, love?"

"Well," I start to consider the trip again. I could definitely use some time away from local paparazzi and LA.

Then suddenly the bald man pipes in again, "Actually, we'll only be there a few hours."

"Really? I thought we'd be there a full day or two. What else is possible?" Ashton asks the man.

The bald man eyes me up and down. I can tell he doesn't like me. "Yeah. I'll see," he says in a condescending tone.

"Do you mind?" I give him an evil stare, "This is a private conversation." I take Ashton away from the helicopter.

"Ashton, look." I stop when I hear his mobile ring.

He whips his phone from his pocket and frowns at the display. "Baby, I'm sorry. I have to take this."

It's Sam Howard, his agent. Sam is the only person in the world that can get Ashton to stop everything and take his call. It was so incredible when he was accepted by the Sam Howard agency. And although it has really given his career a boost, I'm not sure it's making Ashton happy. He has always been a big advocate on following his hearts desires, but now it seems that Sam dictates Ashton's every move.

So it's all wonderful for Ashton's career, but now Ashton is working all waking hours, and when I do see him he's too tired for anything. And now it's worse than it has ever been. When Sam Howard calls, Ashton jumps to answer. He tells me it's his choice to create something really special for the world. And whenever he says it I think—really special for whom?

Finally, I hear him say, "Sam, I'll call you when we get on the jet in a few hours, I can't talk now." He seems irritated as he places his phone in his back pocket, but then looks up at me with warm eyes.

Slowly he takes both of my hands in his and makes one final plea, "Rachael, come with me, please."

I start shaking my head. "Ashton, we had this conversation. Honestly, I don't want to go with you. I need to be here for Bella, and remember I have weekly appointments with my trainer? It's okay. There is only so much tanning and shopping I can do in Fiji, and I choose not to go on this trip. I love you, but this trip isn't for me. You understand?" I look for him to agree and he doesn't respond, so I continue, "So, I will meet you in Paris in five weeks from today as we agreed. It'll be fine. I'll be there in five weeks," I say positively.

We had agreed to meet at the top of the Eiffel Tower on May fifth at five p.m. Paris-time. He'd be on his way back from Fiji. Actually, I'm secretly planning to go there a few days earlier so I can do some extensive European shoe shopping and maybe see if I can locate Pierre Brock's original Blissful Soles store. Maybe he would be there and we'd have this instant connection. It's a possibility for sure.

"Alright. Remember, I won't have internet or cell phone access where we are filming. I promise I will call you as soon as I can. In case of an emergency you need to contact the office and they'll courier a message to me. Okay?" He pauses and I watch a single tear rolling down his cheek. "I'm really going to miss you."

"Ashton, wait. I need to ask you," I look down and kick a rock with the toe of the stiletto. "Um. I'm curious."

"What is it?" he asks offering a deep compassionate smile. The one thing I know about Ashton is when I need to voice a concern I will always be heard.

"Ashton, did you know Pierre Brock was a supplier for the film?" I respond in an accusing tone.

"I just heard about him helping out tonight while you

were changing. I was planning to tell you, but with all the drama of the change of the trip plans and then our fall it slipped my mind." he replies honestly yet with hesitation. "Awww, sweetie, I would have told you if I had known sooner. You know that right?"

"Thanks," I nod as a heavy drop of rain lands on my forehead. Actually, I don't think Ashton has ever lied to me. I mean there are things he hasn't told me, but they usually aren't important for me to know. One time his agent Sam told him he was on the nominee list for an Oscar, and he didn't tell me. I heard during the Academy Awards when the category came up and Sam whispered it in my ear. I asked Ashton later why he didn't tell me about it and he said it didn't matter, it was a slim possibility. I disagreed and told him how it was a big honor and we should have celebrated the accomplishment. He simply replied, "If I had actually been a nominee it would have changed how people see me in the industry and that would offer more opportunities, but it was simply just a possibility not an actual physical anything that would make a difference in changing lives for people. So, why would I make it matter?" I went to argue and realized that Ashton doesn't make anything meaningful or significant, but my mind still yells: but this is important! I was about to fight for the celebration, but I stopped myself. Instead I just secretly felt impressed by my amazing hubby. Actually, thinking about it makes me wonder if there is a reason he wants me to go to Fiji with him. Maybe he senses something. Maybe he senses me pulling way. Maybe he doesn't trust me here without him. Oh well, I could come up with many conclusions as to why, but the truth of the matter is that I don't want to go and deal with the filming and film crew.

"I'll be fine. It's only a few weeks, right?" I muster up a smile and give him my little cute-eye stare.

"I love you so much," Ashton replies. Rain drops are falling at a regular pace now and my make-up is starting to run.

"I love you, too." I say as the bald man pokes his head out again and starts towards us.

Every time I see that guy anger starts to brew inside me. Ashton often says when you feel anger it often means one of two things. One—someone is lying to you. Two—it's a potency inside that will facilitate great change when you acknowledge it. It seems more like a lie than anything else. I'm not sure what that's about, so I focus my attention back to Ashton.

"Have an amazing trip. I'll see you in Paris," I squeak out as my throat begins to tighten and sadness rises inside me. Without warning tears burst out and start streaming in little black mascara rivers down my cheeks.

"It's not like I'm leaving forever. I'll be back soon." Ashton wipes a tear from my right eye. "I'll see you at the top of the Eiffel Tower May fifth. We'll have so much fun when we reunite."

He kisses me and gives a grand salute with his right hand—which doesn't help because now I am hysterically crying.

"Bye," I choke out.

"Bye, sweetie, I'll call when I can," he replies compassionately with a wave.

I watch as he climbs into the helicopter. A waterfall of tears is dripping to the ground. I can't control myself anymore. Emotions are rapidly and electrically streaming through my body. I am so overwhelmed, I suddenly feel dizzy and disoriented. I see a camera flash and feel the need to take cover, so I speed off to the nearest building entrance. Paparazzi cameras are flashing from every direction as the helicopter takes off. Thoughts of cruel headlines are flying through my head as fast as the rain is falling from the sky. I cover my eyes to avoid the next camera when suddenly my heel is snagged. Suddenly I am falling—

5

Am I Dreaming?

I HEAR A MAN's whispering voice. I recognize it, but can't put my finger on whose voice it is. I ponder this. It's not Ashton—

"You're awake," states the man's voice energetically.

My head is foggy. I feel woozy. This could possibly be the worst hangover ever. I start my orientation process. Where am I? Um. I don't know. What happened? I think I fell. What time is it? What day is it? Who is he?

I go to open my eyes and can't see. "Oh my, I'm blind!" I scream.

"Wait," the man says removing a sleep mask from my eyes. "They wanted to keep the light off your eyes while you were sleeping," he explains.

I squint. I see a blur of a person. I fall back in to the unfamiliar bed. Augh. I don't feel so well. "What did you say?"

"Darling, are you okay?" The man with the familiar voice is now stroking my forehead. Where have I heard that voice? I can't quite remember it. I gasp. Suddenly like a dart to the heart I remember. I jolt straight up. Ouch. My body hurts. Suddenly, my brain starts to work, I gasp again internally. It's Jake. The voice is Jake's. Why is Jake here? My head jerks to look at the man sitting on the bedside. It IS Jake. "Darling, how are you feeling?" he asks with concern. Did he just call me darling?

I mentally assess my situation for a moment before I respond. "Actually. Um." I take another breath. "I'm fine. I think. I mean, my head hurts. I feel a little foggy," I say sloppily not quite knowing what I am saying. "Why. You. Here?" I ask with a slurry tongue not sure if I'm making any sense at all.

"You had us worried," Jake responds gesturing towards someone in the hall.

What is he doing here? What is he doing here? What is HE doing here? "Um—where am I? What are you doing here?" I finally mumble with a little more clarity. "Where is here? What I am doing here? What day is it? What time is it? Does Ashton know where I am? Oh, didn't Ashton leave on that flight? I'm confused. What's going on?" I ramble.

"Rachael, stop," Jake interrupts. "You're not making any sense. All you need to know right now is that the doctors say you are going to be just fine."

Jake seems really concerned about me, which I don't understand. Has Jake Green forgiven me? The last time I saw Jake was when Ashton and I were registering for post-wedding celebration gifts at Crate and Barrel. Jake didn't see Ashton, and I didn't tell him Ashton and I had already been married, but I think Katie had told him because he was totally cold. Let's just say it was a little awkward. I'll leave it at that. I tried to hide why I was there, but when he spotted the registry gun he knew. That was the last time our paths crossed until today, and I had thought Jake would never forgive me for our sudden break-up.

"Rachael, do you remember what happened?" his question breaks my thoughts, and I snap back to this present painful moment.

I try to force my aching head to think. And after several minutes I mumble, "Yes. I slipped and hit my head after the helicopter flew off. The stiletto heel was stuck. I think. How are my shoes?"

I see a half smile from the side of my right eye.

I touch my head. Ouch. I can feel the bandage on my forehead. "How bad is it? Will I have a scar? Will it look bad?" I ask.

"Probably for a time, but it will be your heroine scar like Harry Potter's," Jake responds touching just below the bandage between my eyes.

I prop myself up on my right elbow to get a better look at my surroundings—which is, ouch, painful. I allow my eyes to gaze around the room. I am in a hospital. The walls are plain. There's a bed next to mine, but no one is there. Jake looks great. He's thinner, tan and wearing a really nice suit. Finally, I look at my body. I lift my gown and find a bandage on my knee and a scrape on my right hand, but other than that my body below the neck looks intact.

"You are at Cedars-Sinai hospital," he finally says and takes a deep breath, "Darling, rest. You had a big blow to your head. The doctors said you might be a little disoriented and confused for a day or two," Jake responds with concern taking my hand.

"Where's Ashton? Did someone call him?" I ask plainly pulling my hand from Jake's grip.

Before he answers I hear a young girl's voice, "Hellooo." She is standing at the door motioning for Jake. She has beautiful long brown hair and looks about five years of age. Jake lifts his hand as a signal for her to wait.

He stands and lovingly moves a piece my hair out of my eyes. I jerk away. "I'll be right back, darling," he says.

I watch as he walks to meet her and closes the door behind him. I hear them whispering in the hall but can't make out a word.

While he's gone I survey myself from head to toe. My head is very foggy. I have a headache. My right forearm feels bruised, but I don't see a bruise. I am a little confused. Scratch that—I'm a lot confused. What's going on? These are all things I can deal with, but what I can't deal with is the fact that Jake is here and not Ashton. I have to know why Jake is here. And why he's being so nice to me after all the crap I put him through. Honestly, I wouldn't be man enough to be this kind it if I were him. I mean, he was expecting to be my husband and then one day out of the blue I leave. And then a few days later he hears that I'm married to someone else.

A few minutes later Jake returns. "Darling, your vital signs look great, they say you can leave this afternoon." He points to a bag on the guest chair, "Your clothes are on the chair in that bag. Why don't you get dressed and you can rest at home tonight," he smiles. When I hear his words I realize Jake hasn't changed too much. He's always spoken in these formal ways—almost robotic. I'm not sure if it's the lawyerly exterior or just plain boring Jake.

"I'm sorry, what?" I actually heard every word, but can't quite comprehend him when he calls me darling. I guess that's just a habit from dating so long, and I'm definitely ready to go home and sleep this off.

"Get dressed. I'll be with Christina in the waiting room," he pronounces coldly and leaves me alone to get dressed. It's at that moment I am so grateful I left him to be with Ashton. Ashton never speaks coldly to anyone.

"Okay," I nod dismissively. I'm ready to leave. I would rather be anywhere than in a hospital bed, especially one where Jake is by my side.

As soon as Jake is out of sight, I take a painful leap to the plastic bag of clothes.

I take a deep breath and yank open the bag, and before I can stop myself I let out a loud, "Oh shit!" I clasp my right hand over my mouth. Did I say that out loud? This is not my stuff. What I see is unspeakable. I'm mortified. Where are my hip sixties clothes? My linen Tahari dress? My Blissful Soles? My phone?

The nurse rushes in, "Is everything okay, Mrs. Green?"

"I demand an explanation. These are not my things." I scream angrily throttling the bag at the nurse—ouch— which I think hurt me more than her.

"Mrs. Green, I am certain that these are yours. We have a strict and standard protocol when it comes to personal belongings."

"Mrs. Green?" I say under my breath staring at the

contents in the bag. What's going on? Did Jake admit me to the hospital as his wife? Why? Well, I know that I'm ready to go home and if I alert them of this incongruency I know they will force me to stay. I open the bag again and yank out the Gap jeans. "Um, never mind. I guess I didn't remember wearing these. My bad," I say lightheartedly.

"Maybe you should lie down," the nurse gestures to help me on the bed.

I jerk away. "No. I'm fine. I just forgot what I was wearing. People do that sometimes you know." I take a breath and straighten my hospital gown as if it were a dress. "Really, I feel fine. I'm fine." The last thing I want is to be stuck in this hospital or a looney bin. "Could you please get me some water?" I say sweetly changing the subject.

Once the nurse has left, I rumble through the woman's purse I found in the hospital clothing bag. Thank goodness—my iPhone! I switch it on and ask Siri to call home. Maybe Silvia will be there. I'd love to hear her voice and see how Bella is doing. The answering machine picks up and says, "You've reached the home of Jake and Rachael Green." Holy shit. Wrong number. This can't be my phone. I scroll through the contacts and only see two recognizable names. Jake and my ex-best friend Katie. I stare at Katie's number. Omigod, I haven't talked to her in years. I wonder how she is. She was mad at me when I broke up with Jake and we stopped going out together. All the feelings of our last confrontation come rushing back. Well, I can't call her. Dang, I don't even know Ashton's office number. I had it programmed in my phone—.

The nurse interrupts my thoughts and hands me a very small plastic cup of tap water. "Do you need anything else?"

"No. I'm fine. I feel much better now. Thank you very much," I say swallowing down a large gulp of water.

I sit there staring at the ugly clothes. Okay. I'll play along. I can do this. I take a deep breath and place one foot and then the other into the jeans. I button the fly and look down at my tired body in Gap jeans. I feel so average. I let out a yawn and reach for the top. It's a plain, gray UCLA sweatshirt. I carefully put it on. And then I see them—the most amazing sandals. They are breathtaking. They are casual yet classic. They are exactly what I would have designed back in school. Actually they are very similar to my award-winning college design. Where did these come from? I slide one foot in. I gasp. A perfect fit. They fit like Cinderella's glass slipper. As I fasten the leather strap, I giggle slightly when I read the embroidered name Sinder Ella Soles. That's too perfect. Where did these come from? I must be dreaming.

I finish dressing and look to see if there is anything else in the bag. I can't believe my eyes. I see an enormous diamond ring. It must be five carats. I pick up the ring and examine it. Cut: teardrop. Clarity: Yes. Carat: Wow. I don't remember the other Cs. I place it on my left ring finger and admire it for a minute. Ashton and I have matching platinum diamond bands but sometimes I secretly wish I had a big rock like this. Rachael Green is a lucky girl.

Once I'm completely dressed I dangle my legs off the side of the bed admiring the sandals on my pedicured feet. I think back to the last time I had a pedicure—well that's the same. This has to be one of Ashton's silly jokes. Alright. I'll play along.

A few minutes later the little girl with Jake wanders in

and sits next to me. She offers me a hug and then says, "I'm sorry your head hurts."

"Oh. It's okay. It'll heal. It really doesn't hurt that bad," I respond back in my childlike voice. I love kids.

She looks towards the door and yells happily, "Daddy, she's fine."

Daddy? Well, this is getting interesting. Jake's a daddy? Where's her mommy? And why is Jake taking his daughter to a hospital to see his ex-fiancé from five years ago? I want to ask these questions, but more importantly I just want to go home and sleep. I'm exhausted.

Jake walks in and sits next to her saying, "See. I told you she'd be fine."

He scans my body and finally says, "Rachael, are you ready to leave? I have signed your release papers."

"Thank you?" I respond with a question.

Jake is dangling his car keys from his right hand ring finger. I look hypnotically at them. That's a Jaguar key. He drives a Jag? No. He's not cool enough to drive a Jag.

He looks me up and down and then says with some concern, but mostly in a Jake robotic tone, "Rachael. Are you okay?"

"Um. Yes. Of course. I'm fine," I say lightly. "I'm just tired," I yawn. I have images of my down comforter, fluffy pillows and Egyptian cotton sheets and can't wait to get home and wake up from this terrible dream.

6

Home?

AN HOUR LATER, we approach Jake's place. I've been asleep nearly the whole time but it's clear we are near Malibu. I look up in shock. We are entering the front gate and in the distance I see an enormous mansion. Without a word Jake floors the accelerator and I'm pressed back in my seat. I spot a row a palm trees standing along the private drive with a swimming pool sparkling behind. The mansion is built in the Malibu hill.

As Jake presses a button above the rearview mirror a garage door opens for his majesty. Now I know this is a dream. I tap my head. Ouch. It's not a dream, and if it is, it's a very painful dream. Yes. Very painful in many ways.

This has to be an elaborate joke that Ashton has fabricated. He's the only one I know who has this kind of creative imagination. Okay. Fine. I'll play along.

Jake parks in the enormous garage and while he's unbuckling he looks at me and says, "You seem to be a million miles away. How are you feeling now?"

I yawn. "Oh, you know. Sleepy, but I'm fine." I reply trying to convince myself as well as Jake. However, I have to admit inside I'm screaming What the hell! Why are we here? I just want to go home—my home with Ashton.

Jake tells Christina to run into the house and grab an ice pack from the freezer.

I reach for the seat belt. "Wait, let me give you a hand," Jake says helping me.

Jake comes around and opens my car door and helps me out. We walk through a garage filled with his jet skis, scuba gear and water ski equipment and then into the house.

When I enter the house I spread my arms and yell, "Surprise!" There is no response, and Jake and Christina are staring at me as if I'm out of my mind—which I agree might be a possibility. I have no idea what's happening.

"Rachael, why don't you go to the bedroom and lie down?" Jake says. "Unless you would rather eat first?"

I shake my head and I stand there dumbfounded. As I stand there Christina shyly hands me the ice pack.

"Thank you," I say to Christina taking the ice pack to my head and looking for her to tell me how I can find the master bedroom. "Well?" My voice is faint but still offers a slightly frustrated attitude. I look up to Jake waiting for him to jump in and deliver the directions, but he doesn't. I open my mouth and then close it again. I can't get my head around this. Am I Rachael Green? His wife? Is what I remember as my past not my past? What's really going on here?

I take a deep breath, and for a split second consider telling Jake the truth. Or at least what I remember to be true. Then after a moment of thought I decide confrontation might not be a good idea while my head is throbbing. So instead, I start walking around the mansion looking for a place to crash.

Along the way, I see five family pictures and I'm in all of them. I stop and look carefully. Those have to be photoshopped. Right? Then suddenly, terror kicks in. What if I am trapped here? What if I'm trapped with this family? What if this is my life from now on? What am I going to do?

As I mindlessly wander into what I believe is the master bedroom, I find myself surveying my memory banks for some kind of evidence that I don't belong here. Evidence that shows that Jake is not my husband and that my real life is with Ashton. Maybe my life isn't a dream, but the thought of being with Jake is a death sentence.

I continue my exploration and I discover I am still fluent in French. I speak a little to myself just to make sure it's true. How could that be? I mean if I didn't live in France for six months while Ashton was shooting *The Traveler*, I wouldn't be this fluent in French—right? There's some evidence.

I also discover that I can name and physically recognize up to fifteen fashion and shoe designers—and not one of them is Sinder Ella Soles. This also makes me question why I would be leading a life in plain Jane, boring, and conservative jeans. I mean what would be the point of knowing all these designers if I didn't wear designer clothes? It doesn't make sense.

"Rachael." I hear from somewhere. I look around. Is it God? Maybe this is a dream after all. "Rachael." The voice pauses. Hmmm, it sounds a little like Jake. "Rachael?" I jump back in fright when I hear Jake's voice from above. He sounds as if he wants me to answer. "Hellooo—" I yell into the air. "Hello?" There's no answer.

"Rachael?" he calls again from somewhere. I see a small box that just lit up on the night stand next to the bed. Ah hah. I walk over to the box. I press the button that says Talk. "Hello?"

"Rachael. Thank goodness you are okay," Jake replies.

"Oh. Yes. I'm fine. Just resting," I sing as if this altered reality is my reality.

"I have some dinner ready for us. Do you want me to bring some up to you or do you want to come down?" he asks politely.

"Neither. I just need to sleep," I say with a yawn, hoping that's the last I hear of Jake for a while.

Before I can flop back on the bed I catch a glimpse of Ashton's picture in a half opened magazine. What? Dully and dispiritedly I sit on the bed with the magazine. I read the blurb. "Number 97. Ashton Hunt. Ashton Hunt, a Los Angeles-based actor and producer, is best known for his films *Forces of Nature*, *The Traveler* and *City of Synchronicity*." What is this? I flip three pages forward. It's People magazine's 100 Richest and Sexiest Men list. Of course it is. My eyes trail down the page and I see number four. It's Jake. Jake? He's not sexy? The blurb reads, "Estimated wealth: $250 million. Founder of Green, Cruz & Associates, LLC, their major accounts include Intel, Sun Microsystems and HP." Two hundred and fifty million and he heats up his own dinner in a microwave? And his wife wears Gap jeans? What a loser! You would think he would be more creative than that.

Then suddenly my mind stops. Wait a minute. What was that? Cruz? My ex-best friend Katie Cruz? She did go to law school. No, couldn't be. Could it?

I let out a yawn, lay my tired head down on the bed comforter and feel a big cloud of depression envelop me. I could have been so much more. How did I end up a trophy wife to a movie star? Actually, now I don't even know whose trophy wife I am. Tears roll from my eyes and drip on Jake's unimpressive cotton comforter. He's rich beyond belief. He sleeps on a cotton bed comforter and heats dinner in the microwave. What a sad life Jake and Rachael Green lead. Ashton would have never allowed this comforter to touch his body—and he definitely wouldn't sleep under it. Ashton treats his body, himself and others around him with beauty, love and kindness. In fact, he infuses everything with love and fun—including everything in our home and life environments. Thinking back, I realize every party he has ever hosted has been elite beyond belief, from the hand designed invitations to table decorations and live entertainment. And the most impressive quality about Ashton is his desire to live life. It's an art to him, and because it is he really lives. I drift off to sleep thinking about Ashton and feeling so grateful to have him in my life—or at least the memory of him.

7

Delusion

THE NEXT MORNING I WAKE to my ringing phone. As usual I start my orientation process. Where am I? What happened? What fun adventures will I have today? Oh, right, I'm at Jake's place. Augh. Screw that. What fun adventures are possible today? I slowly reach for the phone. My body feels as if it has been run over by a freight train—honestly I feel as if I'm trapped under the train, especially when I see Jake sleeping soundly next to me. I hear the ring again. This time the phone wakes Jake. He gives me a sleepy look and I realize he's still the same uptight Jake that I left five years ago.

"Rachael!" he yells angrily at me.

"Where is it?" I say back but not directly to Jake.

"Chair. Purse. Pocket," he responds clearly.

Ah. There it is. I see it. I painfully launch myself on it with secret hope that the person on the other end of the line will give me some perspective about this situation.

"Hello. Hello," I anxiously greet the caller.

"Rachel, it's Lucy," announces a female voice on the other end of the line. I wander into the bathroom and shut the door to allow Jake to sleep.

"Lucy?" I say as I scan my memory banks. Do I know a Lucy? I don't know a Lucy. Ah. Oh. Of course! I recognize that voice. It's Lucy from wardrobe at the studio party. Of course, she's my angel. "Lucy!" I squeal with delight.

"Listen, I know it's early, but we need you here. We are having a little crisis with the Hilton order. Can you come in now? Please. Please. Please," she begs.

"Um. Yes. I guess. Are you still at the studios?" I ask.

"Studio? No. I'm at the Sinder Ella office. Duh!" She says with sarcasm as if I'm supposed to know.

"Okay. What's that address?" I ask with my own little attitude.

"What are you talking about? I'm at the Sinder Ella office," she pronounces with arrogance.

"Oh. Okay. Alright. Thank you. I'll see you soon." I swallow as I press the end button before she can respond with yet another question I can't answer. The last thing I want to do is alert anyone that there's something—um, well—really wrong with me. I have to figure this out fast. I despise the thought of sleeping with Jake another night, but I would rather be here than a psyche ward! Geesh, this story would sound insane. I can hear Jake now: "My wife woke up in the hospital after her fall and now she believes she's been married to movie star, Ashton Hunt."

Suddenly I hear myself in the Talking Heads song, *Once in a Lifetime*: You may find yourself in a beautiful house with beautiful, um, sandals. And you may ask yourself, well, how did I get here? This isn't my beautiful house. You may ask yourself, am I right or am I wrong? You may say to yourself, my God! What have I done?

Okay. Breathe Rachael. Let's find Lucy. Does she have answers that she couldn't tell me by phone? Okay. Take a breath. Now, where's this Cinderella office? I look down at the sandals. Oh, could it be "Sinder Ella"? I open the browser on the phone and search for Sinder Ella in California. I don't expect to find anything, but to my surprise there is a Sinder Ella Soles office in Malibu just minutes from here. I stare at the address in shock and then I toss the phone on the chair.

In a daze, I feel fear shivering up and down my spine. What if Lucy doesn't remember me from the studio party? What if I say something that alerts her that I have lost my mind? I consider not going for a moment, and then I hear one of Ashton's mantras in my head: lack of action sparks a lack of being. And now more than ever I can't afford a lack of being. That's all I have left.

I mindlessly wander into the room-size closet. I stand there contemplating what to wear, and admit to myself that I actually am slightly excited to go to the Sinder Ella office. Maybe I will see some of the new designs coming out this year.

I select a plain and sleek Banana Republic blue dress as it matches the hottest rockin' Sinder Ella sandals in the world. Wow. Her shoes are beautifully lined up one next to the other. I delightfully stare at each one and I can't help but think, two-hundred-and-fifty-million and this poor girl doesn't have a shoe closet for these beautiful things. This can't be real.

Suddenly, I feel as if I'm being watched. I quickly swerve around. There is no one there. I can't help wondering if the paparazzi have followed me here and they're now documenting every step I take. What if this crazy mix-up hit the tabloids? What would happen to me? What would happen to Ashton? I look around one more time and instead of seeing a cameraman, my eyes find another shelf of beautiful shoes. I like Rachael Green, or whatever her real name is. She really does have a sense of shoe fashion. I'll give her that.

I've never seen this brand of shoes in my life but I absolutely love, love, love them. These are made with the finest leathers, stones and colors I've ever seen. And what really makes them so impressive is their delicate uniqueness, embossed words and ribbons. If you were to take all the best features of all the finest sandals around the globe and put them together, you'd come close to these amazing things. I place a pair to my face and take a deep whiff. Wow. If I were a shoe designer, this is exactly what I would create—different , beautiful, elegant, hot. Just like these precious ones that smell of rich sweet leather.

"What are you doing?" Jake asks watching me remove the sandals from my nose and quickly hide them behind my back.

"Oh, nothing. I'm just choosing which pair I will wear today," I say lightheartedly.

"You aren't going into the office today. Are you?" Jake asks with concern.

"Um. No. I was going to meet Lucy at the Sinder Ella office," I pause with the realization that the Sinder Ella office might be my office. "I mean. I feel fine. I'm just going to see what she needs." I ramble to defend my position. I'm not even sure what I do at the Sinder Ella office.

"Oh," he looks down avoiding eye contact. "Are you sure you can make it there okay? Do you need me to drive you?"

"Um," I stand there contemplating that question for a moment. On one hand, if he were to take me I wouldn't have to figure out where I'm going. But on the other hand, the idea of spending another car ride with Jake is plain yucky, plus I don't want him to catch me in my delusional mental state. That could be disastrous. So I resolve to Google it and follow the GPS. I finally say, "No. It's fine. I'm fine, really! Jake, you don't have to worry about me anymore. I'm fine." I speak confidently, but inside I'm not convinced.

After a quick shower, I get dressed and slap on some generic eyeliner and lipstick that I found in the purse. Once my ensemble including hair and make-up is all put together, I stare at my reflection. Actually, I look pretty good. I mean I look really good despite the head bandage! And being that the rest of my life is a disaster, looking good is all that really matters right now! So with that little bit of goodness, I take a deep breath, drop the phone in the purse and start my journey towards this mysterious Sinder Ella office.

I start with a trip down the corridor to the kitchen, where I see Jake again. He nods as if to approve of my fashion ensemble—like I need his approval.

"Coffee?" He asks.

"Yes, please," I respond with extreme delight.

"Milk and sugar?"

"Um. No. I drink it black?" I respond with a question wondering why he doesn't know how I take my coffee.

Actually, I shouldn't be drinking coffee at all. My nutritionist has me drinking this nasty alkaline type of coffee, but I sneak a cup of black coffee every chance I get. One time I actually brought a Starbucks cup to my appointment and she yanked the drink from my hands spilling my precious venti latte on the floor.

Now when Jake hands me the cup of coffee, I feel blessed and overwhelmed with gratitude. I smell the aroma first and then slowly take the tiniest little sip in an enormous bout of joy and delight. "Yum," I whisper as I give Jake a deep smile.

"Good?" Jake asks.

"Yes. Yes. Yes," I respond almost orgasmicly.

"It's Hawaiian Kona," Jake replies. "I know you like a good cup of coffee."

I suddenly find myself questioning everything. Why did Jake ask if I wanted milk and sugar? Wouldn't he know how I took my coffee? In fact, wouldn't he just assume or not assume I wanted coffee? Ashton has always said—question reality, you never know what's limiting you—I just never thought this would be the reality I was questioning.

"I do." I respond sitting at the kitchen table.

"I remembered you liked Kona, so I brought some home from Hawaii," he replies placing a plate of scones on the table in front of me.

I stare at them emotionally rebelling against the carbohydrates and fats. Another forbidden food from my nutritionist.

"Scone?" he asks taking a large bite and munching on it as he prepares a bag lunch. Now, that's something Ashton would never do. You would never catch him preparing a bag lunch or eating while he's doing anything else for that matter. Ashton always eats at a table and savors every single bite.

I stare mesmerized as Jake pulls Wonder Bread from the pantry. That better be for Christina. He takes out four slices. I gasp as he opens a jar of extra creamy peanut butter. What is he doing? Doesn't he know that's horrible for you? And then to my horror, I see him put a knife in a jar of high fructose corn syrup jelly and slap it on the bread. Oh my.

He looks at me and says, "So, Lucy seemed eager to see you?"

"Yes. I know. I better go." I reply not knowing what else to say. So, I take one last gulp of coffee, place the mug down and turn to look for some car keys.

"Wait," Jake says. I turn towards him hoping for some sort of insight. "Take a scone with you. You didn't have dinner. You should eat something."

"Okay. Thank you." I wrap the scone in a napkin and place it in the jacket pocket where I also find car keys to the BMW in the garage.

Twenty minutes later, I arrive at the office building designated by Google maps. The sign reads, "Sinder Ella Soles." It looks like a crystal castle. It is small but elite. I smile with delight as I open the door. The room is filled with shoe art, from framed hand drawings to magazine covers and articles.

As I walk in Lucy thrusts her mobile phone in my face. She's wearing a tight black sleeveless top and a cute tartan mini skirt with a magazine rolled up under her left arm. She shakes the phone in my face as screeches, "Hilton's rep is on the line. She needs to know about Friday, and Pierre is waiting for you in the conference room," she speaks at top speed.

I whisper back, "Lucy, I need to speak with you about the studio party."

"I'm Gaby. Not Lucy," she angrily adds as she shakes the phone in my face.

Gaby? Well, how the hell was I supposed to know? She looks identical to Lucy. I clasp my hand over my mouth with a sudden realization. I remember. That's where I had seen Lucy. Lucy and Gaby are Pierre Brock's twin daughters. I knew she looked familiar. I guess I wasn't used to seeing one without the other. Wait. Did she just say Pierre is in the conference room? I must be in a dream. Gosh, it seems so real.

Oh. Right. I take the phone, "Hello?"

"Rachael, I need to know if you can complete the white braided diamond sandals by Thursday. Ms. Hilton wants them for her gala on Friday. Yes? Or no?" the woman desperately asks on the other end of the line.

"Um. Yes. I guess. Yes, we can do it," I say without thinking and in the conclusion that it doesn't matter as this is just a dream—right? I throw the phone back to Gaby as if it's a hot potato.

She catches it and begins walking top speed down the corridor.

"Wait. Stop. Where is Lucy?" I say breathlessly chasing after Gaby.

She opens the door to a large boardroom where I see this gorgeous forty-something year-old man sitting with a bunch of shoe sketches scattered all over the table. It's Pierre Brock. I stare at him dumbly.

"Oh you found her," he comments peacefully with a big joyous smile.

For a few moments I can't speak. I can't move. I watch as Gaby drops the magazine on the table. "Page five," she says with a smug tone.

I stare aimlessly watching him take the magazine off the table without looking at it and drop it in the trash bin. "Gaby, I don't read this media gossip crap. It's rubbish and kills creativity."

"Fine, but—," Gaby pauses disapprovingly and snatches the magazine from the bin.

"Good morning, Rachael," Pierre says brightly, ignoring Gaby's behavior.

Gaby turns to me and with a condescending tone says, "Lucy is in the warehouse trying to find supplies for the Hilton order." She tilts her head to the boardroom. "Pierre needs to speak with you," she states. "Now!" she adds as she walks out of the room.

My heart flutters as I stare dumbly at him sitting cross-legged just feet from me. A dart of adrenaline rapidly flows through my veins. As if in slow motion, I hear my brain thinking, Pierre Brock: the world's most amazing shoe designer. I can feel a lump is forming in my throat. I am star struck. He is seriously good-looking. He has dark brown slightly graying hair on the temples and piercing blue eyes. His shoulders are incredibly broad and he looks absolutely amazing in his pin striped hand-tailored suit. Actually he looks sort-of like George Clooney if you tilt your head to the side and squint slightly. I gasp as his beautiful eyes meet mine.

"Rachael, are you okay?" he warmly asks. His voice offers a deep sense of caring. I'm sure he's probably wondering why I'm dumbly standing there like a deer in the headlights.

"Um. I'm sorry. I had a fall." I point stupidly at my forehead. "Yeah. I, um, feel a little woozy." Suddenly without warning my knees begins to crumble beneath me.

Pierre rescues me with a rolling chair. "There you are. Sit down." His jaw is strong and his voice is deep and sophisticated. Am I drooling?

I watch as he pours a glass of orange juice from the pitcher on the conference table. I hypnotically gaze at it as he hands me the glass.

"Thank you," I respond in a silvery, dreamy tone. Thankfully, I'm not drooling yet. I check my lip just to make sure.

As I put the juice to my mouth I hear, "Pierre, call on line two. Pierre you have a call on line two." I jump and completely miss my mouth and spill orange juice on my dress. He reaches for the line as I reach for a napkin. We knock heads in the exchange.

"I'm so sorry." I say in embarrassment as Pierre answers the line. He nods to acknowledge my apology.

"Pierre Brock," he says to the phone.

While he's talking I gaze at him feeling slightly paralyzed. My heart gives a little leap when I hear him mention Prada and Jimmy Choo. I have often imagined having a business in the same league as these amazing designers. How exciting for him.

As his conversation continues I can't help but feel grateful to be in his presence. As Ashton would say, How did I get so lucky? I have to admit that it was totally worth having to wake up next to Jake.

I remember the first time I was introduced to his designs. It was in Napa Valley—Ashton and I had been married several months and we took a weekend road trip. After several winery stops we arrived at one where I saw a woman wearing these fabulous leather strappy sandals. She had strolled over to the car and asked Ashton for a ride in his new yellow Lamborghini. I was a bit tipsy and jokingly said, "He'll give you a ride, for your sandals." She hesitated and then responded in a flirting tone to Ashton, "Why not. You'll make it good, right?" This triggered me at first, but when I saw her taking off her sandals to give them to me, my eyes widened with joy. I was deeply in love with them and Ashton knew it. I remember him saying that my shoe-love was worth taking a stranger for an innocent ride.

I dimly hear Pierre say to the phone, "She's right here. I'll tell her now. Thank you. Ciao. Ciao. Ciao." What? I look up not knowing what's going to happen. He places the receiver down and stares at me. I can feel excitement brewing deep inside him.

"Are you feeling a little better?" he asks with a smile breaking through.

"Oh, yes. I'm feeling much better. Thank you." I respond slowly, anxiously waiting to hear what's happening.

"Well, guess what?" He looks directly in my eyes and I can tell he's bubbling with joy. "We're going to Cannes the first week of May!" He pauses and waits for some response from me. "Rachael, your design was selected, and we've been awarded a slot for a special Sinder Ella Soles runway show at Cannes Fashion Week."

"Oh," I pull a face and out of my mouth comes, "We? Me? What?"

"Rachael, it's true. Did you hear me? We are doing a runaway show during Cannes Fashion Week!" He's now beaming directly into my eyes. "We are going to shake up this world with inspiration, consciousness and fabulous shoes!" He opens his arms for an embrace and says, "I love you so much."

I stare at him unable to speak. Early May? With a jolt my head snaps into full throttle. Ashton. Paris. May fifth at five in the evening. I wonder what Ashton is doing now? I should have gone with him to Fiji. I always make the wrong decisions.

"Rachael?" I hear Pierre in the background behind my thoughts.

My head doesn't stop. What's going on? What's he talking about? Did he say I love you? Cannes Fashion Week? Ohmigod, I feel dizzy. Nausea starts bubbling from deep inside and now my world is starting to spin.

"Rachael, what's wrong? Imagine the impact we'll have on the world. Sinder Ella Soles is now an internationally-known line. Your line! This is what you've wanted, isn't it?" he says trying to make a genuine connection.

"Um. My line? Yes. Absolutely." I squeak out slowly as I nearly fall off my chair. "I'm not usually this clumsy," I say as blood rushes to my face. I stare at the table to get my bearing. My eyes are seeing blurry drawings of shoes, some snaps, buckets, materials and a bowl of some raw cashews and almonds. I lunge for the bowl and grab a handful of nuts and start stuffing them in my face. "Erm. I'm not feeling so well. I think my blood sugar might be low," I say with a chipmunk smile.

"Oh. I know you've had an interesting forty-eight hours." He touches my jaw line and brings my eyes to meet his. "I've been worried about you."

I jerk back and nod furiously with a mouthful of nuts. I put a few more nuts in my mouth so I have an excuse to stop speaking.

"Do you want me to order some lunch?" he asks slowly.

"No. Really, I'll be fine," I say with a mouthful.

"Rachael, this is what we have been creating," he pauses, "Why don't you draw up a few ideas? It will make you feel better. Let your creativity run wild. We can talk later about the details." He pushes a sketch pad and pencil in front of me.

I pick up the drawing pencil and observe it as my body stiffens with fright. Who does he think I am? Does he think I'm a creative designer? I'm not creative or a designer. I haven't drawn a single design since college—not a real one anyway. I don't think my doodling now and then counts in the real world. I put the pencil tip on the paper and start to draw a sandal similar to the picture in front of me. Once the toe sketch is complete I stop and look at Pierre. He's watching every line I draw. I secretly love the attention, and I love the idea of being a shoe designer. It's been my life-long dream, but he has me mistaken. I don't want to disappoint him. Playing for time, I finally say, "I need to think about this for a minute. My head is very foggy from the fall. You understand?"

"Of course. Do you want to rest?" he asks. "I didn't realize you were feeling that bad."

I stand up and hear a crash. What?! The table cloth was snagged on the chair wheel. I look up and find the orange juice pitcher broken and Pierre frantically wiping his shirt tail and crotch. I grab a handful of napkins to race over to help.

"Rachael, it's fine." I snap to alert when I realize where my hand is, as it's not exactly in the most appropriate place. In fact, it's smack center in his crotch between his thighs. I am going to die of embarrassment today.

I quickly retreat. "I'm so sorry. I can't believe I did that. I'm so so sorry," I ramble.

"It's fine, Rachael. Go rest. I'll have housekeeping clean this up," he says and kindly gestures for me to leave.

As I open the boardroom door to leave, I immediately see an office to my left marked with the name Rachael Green. Thank goodness. I dash into the room and lock the door behind me.

I look around. There are pictures of me all over the room. In one I'm receiving an award certificate, in another I'm holding up a gigantic shoe trophy, and in yet another I'm in a restaurant with Pierre and his twins Gaby and Lucy. I wander over to the desk and see three sketches on my desk. One says Hilton Idea. I like it. Each braided strap over the toe has five diamonds. And it looks like it has a cute kitten style wooden heel that has etched letters that says SOUL. How cute is that?

I'm staring at it in admiration when I hear a knock on the door. "Knock. Knock. Rachael, it's me Lucy. Gaby said you wanted to see me," Lucy calls from outside the door.

My entire body suddenly relaxes with relief when I realize this is all a big joke and Lucy is here to rescue me. I open the door with relaxed glee. "Lucy, come in. Boy am I glad to see you," I yelp.

Then before she is seated I say, "Lucy, do you remember talking to me at Ashton Hunt's Studio? Don't you remember? I slipped in the rain? Remember, I was wearing a linen dress and red designer leather jacket? Everything was soaked with rain water? You helped me find some new clothes and let me borrow a pair of Blissful Soles. Remember? You remember, right?"

She stares into space as if she is surveying her memory banks. She raises an eyebrow. I see a bit of glimmer as she nods. Yes! I cheer internally. Then she takes a deep breath and shakes her head. No? Now her body language acts as if she has no recollection about what I'm talking about.

"Rachael, I'm not sure what you are talking about." She changes the subject by lightheartedly asking, "Hey. How's the Hilton design coming along? Are you getting happy with it?"

"What?" I reply in a daze feeling my body start to shake in terror. My hands and legs are trembling, my head is spinning and now nausea is exploring every area of my body. I find myself leaning against the wall and sliding down until I'm seated.

Lucy squats down in front of me, "Are you okay? Can I get you something?"

I groan and push her to the side and make a mad dash to the restroom.

8

With No Story Every Step is the First Step

TEN MINUTES LATER I find myself pressing my right temple against the cold stall wall. I can hear Lucy and Gaby whispering outside the restroom door. I listen intently to the conversation. It sounds as if Lucy just said, I bet she's pregnant. Is she kidding? Not! I quietly tip-toe to the main restroom door hoping to hear more when Gaby whispers, "No, she's just confused, because—" She trails off. I hear her being shushed by Pierre. My body still quivers when I hear his voice. Finally, I hear Gaby let out a whiny, "Okaaay."

Once the conversation is silenced, I emerge feeling confused, frustrated, and just plain embarrassed. I see Pierre and give him a half-smile. Pierre smiles back and places his shoulder under my armpit.

"You're sick. Let me take you home to rest," he says.

I nod.

He holds me as we walk through the front entrance to

the parking garage. He doesn't need to, but I have to admit I love the warmth and caring touch I feel from him. I climb in the passenger seat, and as I fasten the seat buckle I let out a big noisy fart. I clasp my hand over my mouth, roll my eyes to the sky and say, "Excuse me. Obviously, my tummy is not happy, today."

Pierre gives me a look as if to say it's no big deal.

Now that I'm up close, I realize he's older than I thought. He must be almost fifty. I take a moment and do the math. If Gaby and Lucy are almost twenty then he's likely at least forty-five. I sit there in awe for a moment. I've always admired his creative work and he's just as I've imagined.

"Do you think this is from your fall?" he asks with concern.

"I guess. Can you tell me what you know about my fall?" I ask looking to put some pieces together about what really happened. I feel happy that I have him alone to ask a few questions. I know I don't really know him, but he seems like someone I can trust.

Unfortunately, before he can respond, his mobile rings and I end up listening to several business conversations—conversations about material, stones and even manufacturing equipment. It's all very interesting and exciting, and for a moment it completely takes my mind off this crazy situation.

Twenty minutes later, we arrive at Jake's mansion. We take a detour through the kitchen and Pierre grabs a box of saltine crackers on our way up to the bedroom. His familiarity with the layout of the house allows me to know that he has been here before, but I don't ask why. I sit on the bed and he hands me the crackers.

"How are you feeling?" he asks.

"Actually, I am feeling much better now," I say as I take a cracker and place it in my mouth. I look directly into his bright blue eyes. "You don't have to stay. I mean, I know you have a lot to do," I say in dismay.

He kisses me on the forehead and sits back, "Are you sure you're okay?" His face looks genuinely concerned. "Well, would you feel better if I stayed or if I left?"

"Stayed, I guess," I look down as I fidget with my hands. "I'm just embarrassed from everything that happened today. I didn't really make a very good first impression. Did I?"

"Rachael, it's okay," he acts as if we're familiar, but I'm not sure why. This isn't my life. I know I don't have a twin. So, what the hell is going on?

"What?" I ask in confusion. "I don't know you, do I?" The words just come out of my mouth.

He looks taken back, "You don't know? Do you? Jake didn't tell you?"

"What? Know what? What? Tell me!" I screech with urgency.

"Jake told me you have a unique type of amnesia called psychogenic amnesia. I've been told it's temporary," he adds.

"No," I sigh. "That's not right. I mean, it's not like that. I don't have amnesia. I remember last week. I remember everything before the fall. I don't remember knowing you. I knew of you. And I remember Jake, but I remember Jake from years ago. I remember everything differently. I don't know what to do," I start to sob. "I don't have amnesia; I just don't remember this life."

"What? What do you mean differently?" He pauses and then says, "You mean you remember some things? Is that right?"

I bite my bottom lip, "No, not exactly." I trail off in thought and rub my right finger along my lip as I compose my next thought. "Hmmm, Jake told you I had amnesia. Why didn't he tell me?"

Pierre shakes his head. "I'm not sure. I'm sorry. I'm not completely sure he really understands what's going on with you. Yesterday, while you were in the hospital he called me and told me that you were fine and needed some rest. I had gotten the impression that the amnesia happened before your fall."

I take a deep breath feeling the tears roll. Then finally I let out whining, "Augh. I don't know what's going on. I don't know who I am. I don't know what I'm doing here. Pierre, what's wrong with me?"

"Rachael, stop. Maybe there is nothing wrong. Would you be willing to just be with this instead of looking for answers—at least for a few days?" His voice is so caring that I don't lash back.

"I guess," I nod with dismay.

"Maybe I can help. What do you remember?" he asks.

"If I tell you, you have to promise to keep it our secret. I don't want to end up in a loony bin."

"You got it, my friend," he nods.

"Okay." I take a deep breath. "Well, here goes. Don't laugh. I remember dating Jake over five years ago. I never married him. I was never pregnant. I never had a daughter.

My stomach flips every single time Jake refers to me as mommy. I'm not a mommy. I don't know Christina. I don't know how to be a mommy," I ramble in a state of panic.

"Okay. Let me get this straight. The last thing you remember was over five years ago? You remember Jake. Well, that's something. What if you didn't have a story? I used to say with no story every step becomes our first step," Pierre clarifies.

"Yeah, something like that." I look down. "You know, I would be okay not having a story, but here's the thing. You are going to think I'm completely crazy." I nod several times for his agreement.

"No, I won't. I would never think that of you. I adore you," he replies kindly.

"I remember my life. I remember a life with the man I married and my doggie," I say without offering too many details. "You see, not having a story would be easier than having a different story."

"I see," Pierre says taking a breath. I find it delightful how he can receive what I'm saying so presently without judgment. "Rachael, what I do know is that when things seem really wrong that's the place when change is really possible, and that choice to change needs to come from within you. So, instead of fighting these thoughts, these stories, would you be willing to be present with this? Would you be willing to be with your first steps?" Pierre asks curiously.

"Yes, I would be willing. I understand being present," I reply.

"Did you tell Jake about your confusion?" he says turning to face me.

"I haven't told him. I didn't want the judgment. If I have to live with him I would like to be really clear about what I say," I say reaching for another cracker. "Maybe we should talk about this later. I'm starting to feel a little woozy," I say with a fidget.

"Well, I'm here if you want to talk it through," Pierre says without moving.

"Okay," I pause. "Well, I woke up in the hospital yesterday with Jake by my side, which was very strange because I broke up with him five years ago. How could I be married to Jake? Come on. I don't even like him." I look down and collect myself. "The truth is, I'm just not sure what is real and what isn't. Are they all just dreams and stories in my head? How could that be? They don't feel like stories. They are memories. I know it!" I feel my anxieties rushing in as I tightly twist a thread from the cheap bedspread around my middle finger.

"Well sweets, I would say go with what feels light to you. I call it following your Knower. And don't get stuck in the conclusion that your memories are the end all be all," he places his hand on mine. "I'm sorry. I know this is a crazy time for you."

"Thank you." I open my mouth and shut it about five times as I try to continue the conversation. I don't know how to tell him I know I have been married to actor Ashton Hunt for the past five years—so I don't say a word.

"Rachael. What is it? Just say it. Tell me," Pierre urges.

"I can't tell you, not now. I don't know you," I finally say.

"Do you not know me, or do you not remember me?" he asks curiously.

"Good point. Yes. I do feel as if I know you, but I'm not going to say." I laugh and ask, "I was wondering," I gulp "What is our relationship?"

"Well. We're business partners and I totally adore you." He pauses as if he doesn't know what else to say. "You've had a long week, and right now you need to take care of you."

I nod, "Yeah. I'm pretty tired."

Suddenly we hear a loud clatter. We both jump. "Ohmigod, it's Jake!" I say feeling as if we are doing something totally obscene and wrong.

He looks left, right and then shrugs his shoulders as if to say I don't know what that was. Finally, he nods and asks, "Are you uncomfortable with me here? I can hide in your closet. I don't think it's Jake, but I definitely don't want to create anymore chaos in your life."

"Yes. Right! Actually, I'll come with you." I smile, "I mean, I should be at work, right? I don't want to see Jake. I don't want to explain why I'm home. And I really don't want to have to lie. I'm a horrible liar."

"Really? You're joining me? Isn't that going to look worse if we're caught?" Pierre asks in confusion.

"I don't know. We won't get caught," I say after a moment of thought.

"Come on. Let's go." He motions for me to follow him. We both tiptoe into my closet.

I can't see a thing, but can tell from Pierre's voice that he's sitting on the floor. "Rachael, what are you afraid of?"

"Just about everything. I'm afraid to be stuck here with Jake. I'm afraid on never feeling joy in my life." I sigh. I sit down next to Pierre. He wraps his right arm around me and I drop my head on his shoulder and off I go telling him my secrets. For some reason I feel comfortable and safe with him.

"What's the value of holding on to all these secrets?" he asks.

"Well, I guess it's to keep up with my facade. Eek. Yeah." I say it out loud—not really wanting to admit it.

"So, if you are the creator of your life, why would you choose this?" Pierre politely and creatively asks.

"Yeah. I get it. It's like I'm not being the creator of my life," I say sadly.

"Would you be willing to unplug from your facade?" Pierre asks.

"Yes." I whisper.

"Awesome. Now, would you be willing to be the creator of your life?" Pierre asks.

"Yes." I whisper.

"Awesome."

We hear another loud clatter. I notice the noise sounds like metal equipment clanking. I've hear it before on Ashton's move sets, "Did you hear that?"

"Rachael, we're safe," he responds with a genuine concern.

"I'm not afraid of being caught by Jake. I'm actually afraid of not creating my life on my terms," I whisper.

"Well said my friend," he smiles.

I suddenly say as if a media headline, "'Rachael Hunt Lost in Time and Space,' I can see it now." I say it jokingly, but inside I feel empowered to really stand up for myself.

Pierre shifts and I can feel his breath on my face. I admit it's a bit of a turn on. "Hunt?" he starts, "Is that your maiden name?"

"Oh. Um. Yes," I mutter. I can't tell him that I actually think I'm married to a famous movie star.

"Rachael, are you really lost? Could you stop looking at who and what you are like being lost and instead follow your Knower and the possibility that lies in front of you?"

I laugh and nod in acknowledgment. I'm about to say that Ashton is a big fan of following the energy in that way, but I stop myself before I say too much.

"So, what can we choose now?" he asks joyfully.

I frown in thought. "Well, we could choose to get out of this closet," I laugh feeling lighter now.

"Let's come out of the closet," he laughs.

"Okay," I say, not quite sure how else to respond. After several seconds of opening my mouth and closing again I say, "You know, it feels pretty good being here with you."

"Good. I'm glad. I'm glad I could help," he replies as he adoringly places his hands at my waist and turns me to hug him.

I look up at him, "So, now I get to choose. What should I choose?" I say stupidly.

"Didn't I just tell you that? You start by being curious about the next fun, joyous, light thing. Then you choose from your awareness. In other words, follow the lightness of energy," he responds with clarity. "Oh, and do this all the time, okay?" he nods.

After a moment of receiving his words I respond with,

"Yes. I'm curious, if you were me, what question would you ask?" I stutter.

"Good question. What do you think it would be?" he teases.

I giggle, "Well, you already asked: What can we choose now? And I received the awareness to get out of the closet," I respond.

"Yeah. I think the coast is clear," Pierre says opening the door. "You know what?"

"What?" I say with my hands on my hips.

"You need rest, and I need to get back to the office," he replies.

"Okay." I respond back superficially.

"Call me if you need anything," Pierre waits for me to reply.

"Of course," I nod.

"I mean it! I'll be at the office. Call me if you need anything or if you just want to talk." He kisses my forehead, "Feel better. I'll text you later to see how you are." He brushes a strand of hair from my eyes and places it behind my right ear.

Together we walk to the front door, and I perceive a warm feeling of gratitude come over me. Thank goodness I have someone who cares. There is this phenomenal person who can really see me for who I am without trying to fix me, change me or judge me. He just sees me—how awesome is that?

9

Without My Role, Who Am I?

Once Pierre is gone, I race back to the bedroom and do a full-body plop on the bed. I lie there feeling somewhat vulnerable—somewhere deep inside I know Pierre's advice opens a door to a different possibility for me. He told me something that I know will change everything. So, I muster up some inspiration inside and choose from what feels light from my inner knower. What I know right now is that the one thing that feels light is Ashton. Everything else feels heavy like a big thunk in my body.

Despite the thunk I allow my mind to ponder possible light ideas and ask a few questions about each one. If this reality with Jake is a heavy lie, what would I choose? Suddenly, I perk up! That's it!

I need some physical evidence. Yes, that is it. That will jog my memory. Of course. Let's see. Where do I look? If Jake and I have actually married, there would be a ton of history in our house together. Right? History beyond a few hanging wall pictures. I must have shopping lists, cards, and letters—there must be something in my writing. I sit up feeling empowered once again.

With an adrenaline rush, I leap from the bed and start hunting for nuggets from our life together. I start opening all the bedroom dresser drawers. I rummage through all kinds of cotton tops, panties, bras and socks—things that I don't recognize or remember. I dig through some old scarves hoping that I hid a love letter or something under them. I find a drawer of jewelry—none of it is familiar.

Twenty minutes later I find myself sitting in the middle of Jake's office in a pool of stuff. I'm going through a pile of Jake's old CDs, DVDs and yearbooks. I put an old eighties Whitesnake CD in his Bose player. I listen as I continue to scour his office for evidence. There has to be a wedding DVD, album, a mix CD, a bank account or something somewhere in this massive place. Right?

Suddenly, I see something gleaming from behind the CDs. I curiously move a handful of them to one side and discover the most beautifully decorated journal I've seen in my life. I think for a moment; this would be something I would have bought. There's a red Chinese dragon made out of rubies on the cover and five diamond stones along the dragon's spine. It is absolutely gorgeous. I know Jake wouldn't buy something like this.

I slowly open the book and find a small tag on the inside cover. I pull it out. It's Gucci. The price is nearly four hundred dollars. I flip through the pages in anticipation, but to my dismay it's blank. Not one word is written. I sigh.

What's this? There's a small linen card placed in the back pages. I pull it out slowly. It's sealed. I fondle it for a moment wondering if I should open it. As soon as I decide to open it, I hear my phone ping.

I jump as if I've just been caught red handed in the middle of a crime scene. I sit straight up and lunge for my phone across the floor. It's a text. Ashton? I think, hopeful. Crap. It's Jake. I stiffen. I stare at the words with trembling hands: **when are you leaving? do you want to meet at moes?**

Augh. I don't want to deal with Jake tonight. I text back: **no not feeling well - you go.**

Which is not entirely true, I feel fine now, but the thought of spending an ounce of time with Jake makes my skin crawl. And I know I don't want to socialize with him and pretend to be his uptight wife. At least when I showed up as Ashton's trophy wife everyone wanted to be me. It was an honor to be admired in that way by the other women.

I place the phone down and my mind starts reeling about my life with Ashton. Or at least the life I thought I had with him. I think about all the parties, movie premieres, traveling, scuba diving, horseback riding and dancing we'd done. It's funny looking back, I used to feel as if I had no choice in what we were doing, but now I remember Ashton always asking me what I desired—sadly the story in my head was just too big to hear him ask. Mascara tears start making smudges on the beautiful journal. I try to hold them back, but my thoughts move back to my last night with Ashton at the studio party. How could I have been so mean? I've spent so much of my time fighting, defending, justifying, resisting and denying every single thing around his career and mine that I forgot to receive his adoring love. If I ever get back with him I will never take him for granted again.

I look at the card from the journal once again. Screw it. I'm not fighting this. I'm opening it. I carefully lift the back flap without ripping the envelope. Once it releases I gently pull out the card. It reads, "Happy Birthday Darling! Love Jake." Wow, I can't believe he actually bought me something this extravagant.

I neatly place the card back in the envelope and put it in the journal where I found it. I consider putting the journal back on the shelf, but I decided to keep it. I mean, I am his wife after all. It's mine.

I open the journal and write my name on the first page. Then on the next page I draw a little infinity sign and start to write a few questions below: *What am I justifying, defending or fighting for?* A helluva lot. Yeah. I am going to let that go now.

I sigh as I think about every time I make an excuse or justification about why I feel inferior to Jake and Ashton. Wow. I feel a floodgate of ease start to come over me like a waterfall.

I take the journal into the master bath. I turn on the water and I place the journal on the sink counter as I strip down and prepare to soak in Jake's massive porcelain tub. The beautiful tub fills with warm water, and I begin to hunt for some bath salts, bubbles and some joyous music. I find nothing. I stare at the scent-less, music-less, bubble-less tub and remember the Bose player I had seen earlier in Jake's office. With a screech of excitement I head down the hall stark naked to retrieve the player. Once it's in my hands and I start back to the bath, I hear another odd clank. I look around, but don't see anything unusual.

I make it to the bedroom and stop dead in my tracks when I hear a male alto voice singing in the master bathroom. Shit. It's Jake. That sound must have been him coming in? He is singing a love song in French. How funny. I snicker quietly listening from the other side of the door.

Then without warning, the door swings open. I lose my balance and find myself falling on a half-dressed Jake.

"Rachael! What the hell? What are you doing?"

I jump back and grab the floor mat to cover up. "I slipped!" I yell angrily. "I slipped, Jake," I say again. "I was getting bath supplies. Didn't you notice the tub was filling?" I shrug. "What are you doing home anyway? It's so good to see you," I lie.

He looks a taken back by my change of tone, "Um. I came home to change my clothes?" He answers me with a question as he puts on a pair of pants hanging from the bathroom door hook.

"Okay. Well, um, I'm going to take a bath now." I quietly ramble in confusion as we both stand there awkwardly.

"Terrific," he says uncomfortably glancing down at the journal.

I quickly launch my naked body into the tub and once I'm settled I see Jake staring at me.

"What? Is there something else?" I ask hoping he will leave.

"Um. Nothing. I was just thinking. Do you want me to turn this on?" Jake gestures to the Bose player now on the floor.

"Yes. Please. Thank you," I say lightheartedly.

"Rachel, do you want this?" he says fondling the journal.

"Yes." I reply finding my heart pounding in terror as if I just stole it from his top secret stash.

"Where did you find this?" he asks.

"Oh. It was behind the old CDs," I say gingerly with a smile as if it's no big deal.

"I see. It's yours," he says in deep thought.

"It's beautiful," I reply feeling more confused by his response. What is he thinking about?

He stands there for another minute just staring at the ground.

"Jake, what is it?" I ask curiously.

"I was just thinking how beautiful you look. You look really good." He comes over to the tub and kisses my forehead. "Have a good evening." Then, in a business-like tone he adds, "Oh, don't forget to pick up a gift for Kate's daughter's party tomorrow night. The party is at five, remember?"

Remember? I don't even know who I am let alone remember anything. And he knows I have amnesia, why would he think I would remember anything. I consider telling him the truth, but don't want to get into it, so I give a yes-whatever-you-say nod.

"It's important. Don't forget," he says again.

"Okay." I respond clearly.

Once he leaves I open the journal and write: Find out who Kate is? How old is her daughter? Does Pierre know?

I hear the garage door close and let out a big sigh of relief. I feel as if I have had my guard up. I'm curious about that. Do I always have my guard up when I'm around others? I open the journal and ask about it.

What guard am I using to keep people out? What is this protective armor all about?

I place the journal down outside the tub and start to replay everything that just happened in my head. I sit there for another minute and grab the journal and start to write what I remember about my life with Ashton. And then I start to write about Jake. I become curious about my relationship with Jake. I mean if this is just amnesia, I'm curious. Do we not have sex? Do we party together? Do we have any fun? It was weird how he called me beautiful. If we are married would he still be saying that? And why did he repeat the information about Kate's party? If I had really known about it, would he really think I would forget? Or does he know I have no idea what he is talking about? Hmmm.

I hear a text message ping. Now what? I emerge from the tub, towel off, wrap my wet locks in the towel and step into a white cotton robe.

Now armed with my phone and journal, I wander to the sitting room's over-sized chair and plop down cross-legged. Oh. I check my phone; it's a text from Pierre:

how's your sweet body feeling?

I stare at it. Butterflies are fluttering through my entire body like they do when you are in love. I'm curious about that. I have adored his designs, but I'm not sure why I feel this way about him. I sit and compose a response. I could simply say, much better or better now that I hear from you, or, I'm feeling fine now—what are you doing tonight? But instead of some cheesy response I decide to phone him.

It's ringing and my heart's pounding like crazy, "Pierre Brock," he answers.

"Hey, it's me," I say giddy with excitement.

"Hi, Rachael. How are you feeling?" he asks.

"Oh, I'm fine. I guess I'm just a little shaken from all the information. Hey, I have some questions for you," I say quickly.

"Go for it," Pierre says.

"Do you know a Kate? Apparently, I have a party to go to and need to get a gift for her daughter. I have no idea who she is or how old her daughter is," I ask.

"I think she works with Jake. Kate Cruz is her name," he replies.

"Oh. Katie. Right. I didn't know she had a daughter. Do you know how old she is?"

"I'm not sure, but I think Katie is your friend. Maybe you could call her and ask what her daughter would like for her birthday," he pauses, "Rachael, why don't you tell Jake about your memory?"

"It just hasn't felt like the right time," I yawn. "I will soon. I better get some food and go to bed. Ciao."

"We'll talk tomorrow. Good night," he replies.

"Good night," I respond.

— Journal Entry —

Who Am I? What Am I?

Being with Pierre excites me. He is very different in this world. He lives in this world in a way I really didn't know existed. He lives without the stories, without necessity and every step follows a natural state of joy.

When I'm around him it's very clear he knows who he is—what he is. He knows this from a place of true being. He chooses what to be, say, do from his knower – those nudges in the gut and those whispers through awareness. He's senses and chooses before they get mixed up in any inner defense, reaction, resistance, or judgment systems—he listens, he inquiries and responds from his knower. Like Ashton, he knows what moves him.

I, on the other hand, am always fighting, defending, judging, justifying, resisting, reacting and denying...

And it's time for me to STOP the fight and be me no matter what others think or judge. It's time for me to stop defending, justifying, resisting, reacting and denying everything. I'm ready to know me, what moves me and be me!

10

Creating

I AM SETTLED IN BED ready to sleep but my mind won't stop. I really don't want to face what might be my reality. It looks great on the outside. I live in an incredible home. I'm married to a multi-millionaire. And apparently I'm a business owner of a thriving footwear company. I have a daughter, friends, good-looking husband—yeah, we'll just leave it at that. This was my dream when I was in college, but now things are different. This isn't what I want. I don't know these people. I want my life. And tomorrow I have to go to a child's party where I don't know anyone, and I don't know who I am. I quietly sigh. Well, I'm no stranger to pretending; I've been pretending all my life—what's another day of validating other people's reality?

Now that I'm here looking back on my life—or what I thought was my life—I realize I have never really been happy with who I was. It seems as if all my life I have been trying to be what someone else wanted me to be. My parents. Jake. Other boyfriends. Ashton. Mmmm. Ashton. It's weird. I don't think Ashton really wanted me to be something I wasn't, but I did it for his fans. Ironically, I'm actually pretending to be someone I think he wants me to be. Oh my gosh! I'm totally doing this to myself. This may be my chance to change this insane cycle. One thing is for sure, I will trust what Pierre calls my inner knower, and I will make choices based on it. Okay. This is good. I am grateful for this awareness. I let out a big yawn and take two deep yoga-style breaths as I fall asleep.

∗ ∗ ∗

It's seven in the morning and I am sitting at Jake's kitchen table writing down some of the insights in the journal.

"Good morning." Jake's greeting startles me and I jump. He's standing in front of me in a fine business suit. He touches my shoulder with a friendly gesture, and it sends uncomfortable chills down my spine.

"Right. Good morning." I quickly close the journal.

"What are you doing?" Jake asks.

"Oh, it's nothing." I hesitate, "Just making a list of a few things I have to do." I flash a big warm smile.

"Cool," he says as he presses the grind button on the coffee bean grinder. Once the grinding has stopped he looks at me with curiosity, "Well, what did you come up with for the party?"

"Erm. Well, let's just say I have the perfect present plan." I bite my lip stalling for a thought. "I will purchase it on my lunch break today."

"That's great. I'm planning to be at the party as well, I can't wait to see what you get," he responds as he adds water to the coffee maker.

"Hmmm," I scramble for an answer, "Great," I say with a big fake smile.

"Hey, Jake. Can I ask you something?" I ask watching him start the coffee maker.

"Sure," he responds.

"Where's the party?"

"Kate's house, of course," he responds with a condescending tone.

And before I respond I find myself getting really defensive. Why is he using that condescending tone with me? I'm about to retort when I realize I have allowed Jake to get to me again. It's almost as if he feels a need to make me feel bad. And just when I'm about to address this with him, Christina wanders in the kitchen. So, instead I acknowledge my feelings and choose to be curious as to why he uses that tone with me.

"Hi sweetie. Can I get you some Cheerios?" Jake asks Christina.

"Yes, please," she responds politely to Jake and sits down at the kitchen table directly across from me. She stares at me for the longest minute without a word.

"Hi, Christina. Did you have a good night's sleep?" I finally say, breaking the awkward silence.

"Hi. Yes," she mumbles under her breath.

Jake places the bowl of Cheerios in front of her and she begins shoveling spoonfuls into her mouth.

Jake looks at me again as if to continue our conversation. I brace myself. Finally he says, "I am playing golf with the guys this afternoon. I'll meet you at the party shortly after five." He pours coffee in an old UCLA travel mug. "I hope you have a good day."

And with that I watch as he kisses Christina's head and comes over to me and places the mug on the table. "You'll be okay? Right?"

"Yes, of course. Just one thing—" I look down at him as I compose my next thought, "Do you have an invitation for the party?"

"No. Why would you need an invitation for Aslyn's fifth birthday party?" he replies.

"I don't know. I just thought I would ask," I say, acting as if I know all the details, while really I'm in total shock. I never even remember Katie dating anyone. I can't believe she has a daughter. There was this one night in college when she woke up in a guy's dorm room after a long night of drinking, but I don't recall her having any other kind of relationship. I wonder if she had a one-night stand.

Jake gives me a look of concern. "Okay. Well, I'll see you at Kate's house on Wilshire around five. Are you okay to drop Christina off at school and pick her up?" he speaks very deliberately—as if I'm deaf. I can tell he's slightly agitated.

"Yes. I will be fine," I mutter under my breath. I know that Christina goes to the Summit Elementary school since I noticed the branded folder she put in her backpack.

"Rachael, are you sure you're okay? That blow to the head must have gotten to you more than we thought," he says dropping a book in his briefcase.

"Oh. Really, I'm fine. I had just forgotten." I say confidently and deliberately hoping he will say something about my amnesia. I mean, if I have amnesia it would be nice if my husband told me.

"Okay. I'll see you later. Have a good day," I reply hoping he'll leave.

"Great," he replies.

Once he's gone I feel an incredible relief inside. It's a lot of work pretending to be someone you're not—whether I'm doing it intentionally or not.

I check my watch and smile when I think of where I'm going—my new footwear business with Pierre Brock. Yes! I cheer internally. Now I understand why Ashton seems so exuberant when he goes to the studio—it's his art. And this is my art. I can't wait to get to my beautiful crystal office. My body is bubbling with shoe design ideas and creative juices. Just thinking about it makes me smile in a way that I just can't hide.

After a few moments of these artistic thoughts, I look up and see Christina staring at me. I realize I better be a mother right now and be a shoe designer when I get to the office.

"Are you excited about the party tonight?" I ask her in a childlike tone.

She nods.

"Do you like Kate's daughter?"

She nods again.

"That's good." I nod several times finding myself at a loss for words. I can't think of anything else to ask her.

You would think she would be dying to share her life with her mother—unless I'm a horrible mother. What if I don't share stories and conversations with my daughter? I take a moment to think about something to share, but all I come up with are stories of our pup Bella, horses and Ashton—all from my other life—so I just keep quiet. I resolve to search the kitchen for some healthy food. I find an apple and some natural peanut butter hidden in the back of the pantry. At one point I even let out a little, "Yahoo," while slicing the apple. My body is craving natural foods. I place the food on the table and eat as slowly as possible hoping this uncomfortable moment with Christina will pass quickly and it will soon be time to take her to school.

I still have the last bit of apple in my mouth when I have a twinge to check my mobile phone secretly hoping Ashton or anyone from my old life will find and rescue me. He'll find me. He'll be my knight in shining armor.

I look up at Christina and see her playing with her food. "We better get going," I finally say nodding a few times. "Do you know how to get to your school?"

She nods.

Thank goodness.

✶ ✶ ✶

By seven fifty-five, I have dropped Christina off at school and now I am opening the crystal doors to Sinder Ella Soles. Despite my awkward morning with Jake, I feel a tingle of excitement rolling up and down my spine. My very own designer shoe company. I squeal quietly. It's a dream realized.

"Good morning," I sing cheerfully to Gaby at the reception desk.

Gaby scowls back and says, "Pierre and Lucy need to speak with you right now, Rachael. Go. Go. Go." She eagerly points in the direction of the boardroom. I'm beginning to realize Gaby is angry and annoyed nearly all the time. I'm pretty sure it has nothing to do with me—it's just who she is. I'm personally not choosing to buy into it. I dance towards the boardroom completely unfazed by her tone, mood and attitude.

When I enter the boardroom, Lucy looks up at me with concern in her face. There is a mess of shoes and drawings strewn everywhere. "Rachael, where is the Hilton model for production? I can't find it anywhere."

"How am I supposed to know?" I reply in total utter confusion.

"Didn't you tell Hilton's rep the sandals would be ready for Friday?" she asks in an accusing tone.

"I'm sure you've heard. I don't remember anything about my life," I say sarcastically.

"I heard. The thing is Rachael, you promised the design to her." Lucy's voice rises with a mix of panic and irritation, "You said they would be done. You do have a plan to actually make this happen, right? You know Hilton is thrilled. She can't wait to wear her newest Sinder Ella sandals to the gala. You need to make this happen."

"Um. Yes." I say as my face colors slightly. "Well, I know we can do it too." I do my best to sound confident, but a part of me wants to run and hide.

"By the way Rachael, she is considering having us work on all her sandal design ideas from now on, so we need her to love these shoes." I can tell Lucy is excited with the prospect. I guess I see why; however, I never really desired to do someone else's design. I always thought people would wear my unique designs.

"Um," I gaze into her world to see if by any remote chance she may have doubts too. Then I remember seeing the sketch in my office, "Hold that thought." I rush next door and find the sketch among the papers on my desk along with the necessary measurements and must-haves. "Here's a start," I say as I re-enter the boardroom.

"Great. We need a complete design in five hours so we can get the shoes through production in time," Lucy states firmly.

My heart sinks. I can't imagine it taking me only five hours to figure this out.

"That's plenty of time, right?" Lucy asks eagerly.

"The thing is, I don't really remember how to design. I've lost my memory." I look to the ground with defeat. Then I take a breath and with a new sense of inner power I look at Pierre and say, "What's the best possible thing that could happen here?"

"Yes. What's possible beyond our mind's view point?" Pierre adds.

"I'll leave you at it. I'm sure you will make it work," Lucy says, not quite convincingly, as she heads out of the room.

"Nice question," Pierre faces me, "So, did our conversation yesterday help you?"

"Yes. You could say that." I grin and nod several times. "It's funny. Not only am I being more curious and asking questions about things when I feel defeat, but I'm becoming aware of so much more."

"What do you mean by that?" he asks curiously.

"Well, I realized that I'm doing things that I think other people want me to do. They aren't even asking me to act that way, yet I'm making up these stories in my head about how I should be."

"Ah. I see. I'm glad you are seeing that. Who are you without the story about who you think you should be?" he asks.

"Maybe more of me," I laugh.

"Will you choose to destroy those stories?"

"Yes," I nod.

"Awesome," he smiles.

Wow. I can't believe the famous designer Pierre Brock is sitting next to me helping me draw shoes for a celebrity.

"What does this need to look like?" I ask feeling extremely present as I place my pencil tip to the sketch paper. Then suddenly, without a comment from Pierre, it becomes clear in my mind. I draw what I know, and Pierre nods with approval.

"The art lies in the question," he says as he points out a few details and asks me questions about each one so I can uncover the best design.

"By the way, Rachael, I forwarded you the finalization documentation for Cannes. I need you to respond to them with your confirmation. They have a tight deadline and they require all parties to personally respond via email by Friday. Can you fit that in today or tomorrow morning?" Pierre asks.

"Oh yes! Absolutely," I reply as I continue a fine line around the ankle buckle.

"The heel height is one and three-quarter inch and the sole is one-quarter inch." Pierre gently takes the pencil from my grip and corrects the proportions. "It's important that we communicate clearly," he says slowly and deliberately.

"I see," I look up and send a flirty adoring smile as I gently draw the pencil back from his hand. It's funny, the thought that my creation will be worn by a celebrity turns me on—and what turns me on even more is this art of co-creation with Pierre.

This dance of intense presence and creation continues through the afternoon. Once we are finished I check my watch. "We have fifteen minutes to spare before our five hour deadline," I announce to Pierre in delight.

"Yes. And you know Lucy will bounce in here very soon," he replies warmly.

"Shall we wait for her?" I smile delighted with our work of art.

"Well, let's check a few things first," he says reaching across me for a ruler, softly brushing my forearm with the back of his hand. Chills rush up and down my spine as he does his analysis and I do my best to contain my arousal.

"Looks good," he says when we hear Lucy approaching the door.

"So, how's it going?" Lucy asks popping her head in my office.

"It's ready," Pierre says, looking her directly in the eyes.

"Really?" Lucy says in surprise.

"Absolutely. See for yourself," Pierre says using his middle finger to push the paper across the table towards her. I can tell he's purposefully teasing her with the finger gesture.

"We added all the criteria, the nice-to-have features in the original sketch sent to us by Hilton herself. We checked and double checked the measurements. We also placed five diamonds from smallest to largest from the outside to the inside of the first strap. Each diamond has a unique color setting behind it to emphasize detail. The sandal will have a one and three-quarter inch heel made of cherry wood as specified," I say with confidence and ease.

I wait for Lucy's response, feeling a twinge of triumph. I find I have this strange need for approval from her. On some level, I think if she was there the night of Ashton's party, I really want her to know that I'm not just a movie producer's trophy wife. I want her to know that I am very talented on my own right. And suddenly I become aware that this is another way I create a head trip to not be the true me. I think back to Pierre's earlier question about who I am without the story and choose to let this one go to.

"Pierre, you have a call on line three." Gaby yells over the intercom. After a pause we hear, "Pierre, Sam Howard is on line three."

Sam Howard? Where have I heard that name? I internally gasp. Sam? Ashton's agent? I've never liked that guy. Why is Sam Howard calling Pierre?

"I'll take it on my office phone," he says. "I'll be right back," he excuses himself.

I look at my watch. I don't want to disappoint Christina. I still need to get a gift, pick Christina up from school and dash across town so we can make it to Katie's party before Jake arrives. What's a good gift for a five year old? What did I play with when I was little? I stop my thoughts when I notice Lucy looking at me.

"It's perfect! I mean it's better than perfect. It's completely inspired! I'm impressed. I love the stitching you chose around the gems. Nice work, Rachael. I think Ms. Hilton is going to love it. It might just be the best sandal design we've ever made," she says enthusiastically and gives a fist pump in the air.

"Really?" I respond in surprise.

"Yes. Really. Great job," she responds. "I'm going to send the design to Ms. Hilton for approval." She takes the drawing and walks out of the boardroom.

"Wow," I delightfully say to myself. I'm in a bit of a daze from the whirlwind of creating as I head to my office.

A few moments later Pierre pops his head in, "That was really great work," he says.

"Everything okay with Mr. Howard?" I ask probing to see what "his" Sam Howard needs. I mean it has to be a different Sam Howard, right?

"Oh yes. Couldn't be better. Are you excited to hear what Ms. Hilton thinks about our design?" he asks.

"Totally!" I nod with wide eyes. "How long do you

think this will be before we hear something?" I ask timidly not knowing the procedure.

"Oh, maybe two or three hours. It'll depend if we can get a hold of her and if she has time to review the design. Do you want to celebrate with a drink while we wait?" he asks.

"No. This is the night of Katie's daughter's party, so I'll have to leave soon." I shuffle in my chair, "I mean I have to leave to take Christina to the birthday party," I mumble.

"Oh. Right. Kate's party. I remember. Well, I'll call you when we hear back," Pierre replies.

"Great. You know I would stay. It's just," I swallow. "I really don't want to let Christina down. You understand, right?" I nod my head up and down slowly hoping he'll join me in agreement.

"Yes. It's fine, Rachael. I will call you when we receive a response," Pierre joyfully responds.

"Thank you," I say deliberately, as if I'm getting permission.

"You've done an incredible job today. Thanks for co-creating with me," he says as we embrace in a hug.

"You're so welcome," I say over his shoulder.

— Journal Entry —

Conscious Creating

When I work with Pierre it's like I'm working with consciousness through Pierre and myself. There is the constant flow of conscious ideas, inspiration and insights. Whenever something didn't seem good he simply inquired about it, then we both were flooded with new possibilities and changed it. It was this beautiful flow all day.

Now that it is time to stop and take Christina to Aslyn's party, I find this flow disappearing and all I can do is ask... what would it take to always be presently in the flow of creative living?

11

Present Time

CHRISTINA AND I ARRIVE at the party fifteen minutes late with a limited edition Barbie in a gift bag with a ton of tissue paper and confetti.

"Hi Katie!" I say giving her the LA-once-over. "Wow. You look great," I say with a big smile and a bright tone as if our friendship had never ended. She really does look good. She's probably lost fifteen pounds since I've seen her last—or remember seeing her. Katie was never fat, but she always carried an extra ten or fifteen making her a size six or eight depending on the month. I have to admit, I've always enjoyed being the skinny one. Today, she looks like a muscular size two, it's impressive.

"Hi Rachael," she responds in a monotone voice making me wonder if there is still some story keeping us from being best friends. "You can put that over there," she points to a pile of presents. "The others are out back," she says looking past me and enthusiastically welcoming the next guest at the door behind me.

I follow Christina as she races to the backyard. She's clearly been here before. She runs to the moon bounce to play with the other girls, and I find a seat in the obvious place where the other mothers are socializing.

I grab the dragon journal from my purse and write: What's the current state of my relationship with Katie? What are the walls she has put in place in regards to me? Have I created them or has she? Do we still have that heart to heart connection or did something happen? I snap it shut, and place it back in my purse.

I look at the other mothers curiously wondering how to connect with them and then look at Christina playing in delight in the bounce house. Then I see another little girl yelling for her mom to watch her do a flip. And another little one running up to her mom showing her the runner in her tights. Wow. I can't help but notice these children enjoying every little moment. They are so present and really alive in the moment. I see Christina step out of the bounce house and run towards me. I pull the journal from my purse and scribble: focused attention and presence, then drop it back in my purse.

"Mommy, I'm thirsty," Christina whines. I realize at that moment that I am Mommy. I like the sound of that. I, Rachael Hunt—or Green, or whoever I am—am Mommy.

"Thirsty, thirsty," she demands as a wave of protectiveness rushes around inside me. She is my daughter. My daughter. I want to give her whatever she wants. I jolt into full alert and focus my attention on her.

"Yes. Let's get you something to drink," I walk over to

the buffet table and pour her a cup of apple juice from the pitcher.

"Rachael? Hi. It's Sara from yoga." I turn to look expecting to see a stranger, but it really is Sara from yoga—the yoga I remember from my old Ashton-reality.

"Oh my gosh, Sara!" I say with an intensity of recognition. "Hi. It's so good to see you!" I say hugging her, and as I do I find myself covered in red juice by a small pigtailed blond beside us. I jump in fright scaring the little girl. She runs to Katie for a hug.

"Oh. I'm fine. No worries," I say to Katie, who's now looking at Aslyn. I turn back to Sara and as I do I find my arm being taken by another woman.

"Hi. I'm Cindy. You better get that out before it stains. Let me show you to the bathroom," Cindy says directing me to the bathroom up the stairs.

"Sara, I'll talk with you in a minute," I yell to Sara seeing her arm also being taken by another woman.

"I think Kate has some Oxiclean to help with that horrible stain. I'll see if I can hunt it down for you," says Cindy.

"It's fine. Really. I don't even like this top," I say gesturing to the ugly button-down blouse I'm wearing. But Cindy doesn't seem to be listening as she's still forcing me into the bathroom. "I'll be back with something to help get that out," says Cindy, determined to help me get the stain out.

I examine the damage in the mirror. This stain is never going to come out. And I don't care. I look in the lower cabinet for a wash rag to get it wet and at least let Cindy know I tried, but the only thing down there is a box of early pregnancy tests. This triggers me to check my watch date. Oh shit. My period is two weeks late—at least if I'm still on track from my life with Ashton. I pick up the box and read the checklist of symptoms for pregnancy. I mentally go down the list. Breast tenderness. Yes. Morning sickness or nausea. Ah. Yes. Feeling fatigue. Yes. I gasp. I read the directions and take a stick out of the box. I proceed by removing the plastic wrap and putting the stick in a steady stream of urine like the box says.

While I wait for the test stick to process, I start dabbing at the red juice wondering what it would feel like to be pregnant and birth a child. I see myself rocking a baby, changing diapers, and breast feeding. Awww. I want a baby. Then I imagine tights, tiaras, curls and pigtails. I imagine playing together on the playground and shopping for cute shoes throughout the years. Ashton has been hesitant to bring children in our lives, but I'm ready. For a moment I start to think of ways to persuade Ashton to start a family, and then I stop and come back into the present moment. Wait a second. Ashton is not here.

I'm startled by a sudden knock on the door. My heart starts pounding as if I've committed a major crime. "Just a minute," I yell looking to see if the test has finished processing.

"Rachael, it's Cindy. I found a Tide pen if you'd like to try it," Cindy yells from outside the door.

"Oh great. Thanks." I crack the door and snag the pen.

I place the Tide pen on the sink counter and check my watch. The moment of truth. I rush to see the stick.

Two lines. Holy Shit. Don't panic. Where is that box? I bet two faint lines mean that I'm not pregnant. I pull out the box and confirm a positive test. Crap. How could this happen? I drop the test in the trash and try to figure out what to do next. I have to admit I feel a little giddy. I'm excited about being a new mommy. I internally cheer. Suddenly a frightening thought grips my heart. This baby is Jake's—not Ashton's. "Oh. No!" Did I just scream that out loud?

"Is everything okay in there?" Cindy yells from outside the door.

I open the door and respond to Cindy, "It's my period. Yuck. This sucks."

She smiles in agreement as we both return to the party and see everyone gathered around the birthday cake. I give a look around the group. I can't find Sara, so I join in the singing.

"Okay on three. One. Two. Three. Happy Birthday to You." Katie says as she conducts us in song.

I hear whispering behind me, "She's pregnant, really?" responds one lady.

My heart gives a leap and I'm about to retort but instead I shuffle to hear better. Another woman pipes in, "I bet it's Jake's."

Well of course it is—who else's would it be?

And then I hear the third woman say, "You're right. I saw Katie and Jake making out in his office last week."

Okay. What is going on here?

The first woman says, "That doesn't surprise me, they are always flirting."

And then the second one says, "Yeah. I was in my office around nine. I went to tell Jake that I was leaving and saw him and Katie kissing."

Holy shit. Thoughts of motherhood have ceased to exist, and now anger is rushing through my head, body and my entire essence.

When the birthday song is complete everyone starts clapping. I'm firing inside as I watch Katie remove each candle and hand it to Aslyn so she can delight in licking the icing off.

Now, instead of relishing in the focused presence and joy of the party, I feel my blood boiling as I glare at Katie. How could she? I might not remember that Jake is my husband, but she should. How could she disrespect our friendship and my marriage in such a cruel way? That bitch! Stop, Rachael. Don't jump to conclusions. Maybe you just need to ask. I'm sure there's a good explanation.

When the last candle is cleared from the cake, Katie's eyes catch mine glaring at her. I watch as she pulls a large knife out from a leather envelope. Is she threatening me? Katie plunges the knife into the center of the cake. I watch as she cuts and distributes the cake pieces to the children first and then the adults. I consider confronting her, but decide to wait for the right moment. The old me would bury this emotion and let it fester for years— maybe a lifetime. But not now. I've changed. I need to know what happened. I remember what Pierre said about even emotional energy being just energy. I think about it a minute and calm myself before I approach her. I repeat some simple mantras to myself: This anger is just energy; Don't conclude anything; Find out what really happened. Hmmm. Maybe this is the reason she was so cold to me. Stop! Don't jump to conclusions I tell myself once again.

Once everyone has a piece of cake, I make my move. "Hi Katie. Great party. You've really done an amazing job," I start. I've learned to always start a possible confrontation with a compliment.

"Yeah. Thanks, everyone seems to be having fun." She looks around the room with a smile.

"Hey Katie, can I ask you a question?" I ask in a casual tone.

"Sure. What is it?"

"Have you and Jake been making out in the office?" I simply ask a question with no emotional charge whatsoever.

"No. No. I haven't," she says defensively as she shakes her head. Her voice moves to a whisper then she says, "Shhh. Not here."

I stand and stare at her without a word. I am waiting for a valid response. She answered and I could just accept it as truth, but we both know she's lying.

"Rachael, it's not what you think," she responds after a few moments of my I-don't-believe-you stare.

"You mean kissing my husband in the office after hours is not what I think?" I ask kindly probing for something more tangible.

She gestures to move the conversation into a private corner in the house. "Look, Rachael. This is a children's party, please respect our privacy. This is not appropriate conversation," she states firmly.

"Katie, look, I just want the truth. I won't make a scene. I just want to know what's going on. Why were you making out with Jake? That's it." I ask in my most genuine, gentle tone.

"Okay. Fine. It's true," she replies.

"And?" I prompt her for more, finding myself becoming angry but not expressing it.

"What? I confessed. What else do you want?" she asks defensively.

"Well, what's the story? How long has this been going on? Do you love him? Does he still love me? What's this about?" I ask for the details.

"Look, can we talk about this later? I will tell you everything. How about I call you tomorrow?"

I don't respond and I simply wait. I can tell she's starting to panic for something to say.

"Well, you haven't exactly been there," she says spitefully.

"What does that mean? Does he tell you that?" I ask looking for answers.

"Oh come on Rachael, cut the crap. You know what's going on." Katie's anger is growing.

"Here's the thing, *Katie*, I don't know what you are talking about. I really don't. I have amnesia or something like that. Jake wasn't honest with me about it and I'm still figuring out all my relationships. It just seems like a whole lot of dishonesty is happening between all of us. I don't desire this to be this way. Do you?" I say thinking that I now sound like Pierre.

"Whatever. We'll talk about this later," Katie says dismissively as she turns and re-enters the party. It's just like her to flee. She ran from our friendship when I changed my mind about marrying Jake and she's running now. Screw it. Katie will never change and I don't want to fight her for Jake. I can raise this child on my own.

"Christina, time to go," I scream in the direction of the cake. She runs to my side.

"What about Daddy?" Christina says as I help her with her shoes.

"Rachael, wait. Wait. Rachael stop. Stop. Don't go." Katie pleads as we prepare to exit the front door. A flow of consciousness thoughts fill my mind: Am I running from my problems or am I choosing this? I am clearly reacting. Yes. If I stay I may not like myself tomorrow. At least by leaving I stop some excess reactive yelling. So, yes, I'm choosing to leave. If I were to truly be in a zero view point, I would see that Katie is defending her action. I would see that she's fighting to be right. And I would allow her to have that view point and choose my next choices based on that.

I take a breath and step out of this contracted mind space and into new possibilities.

12

Out of Control

WHEN I OPEN KATIE'S front door to leave, I'm immediately jolted with a camera flash in my face. Cameramen are everywhere yelling my name from all different directions, "Rachael. Rachael, over here!" My first reaction is to cover Christina. I shut the front door and give Christina clear instructions to walk directly to the passenger side of the car with my coat over her head. She does as she's told, while I use my arm to cover my face from the camera flashes.

Once we are both in the car I look to Christina who seems mortified, "Are you okay?" I ask. "Will you buckle up? When we get to a quiet place I'll get you settled in your car seat."

"Okay. What is this about?" she asks.

"I don't know, but I will find out. Hold on, Christina. I'll get us out of here," I say, backing the car out.

"Wait! I forgot my goodie bag! Aslyn has the best goodie bags!" Christina wails.

"It's fine. I'll get you one later from Miss Kate. Okay?" I back up and squeal the tires out of the drive.

"It's not okay. I want it, now. Please," she cries.

"Christina, not now. Mommy has to get us out of here," I say making another turn through the subdivision.

After a few more crazy turns I look in the rear view mirror, "Whoa. I think we've lost them."

"I hate you! I wish you would just go away!" Christina grumps.

"Christina, I'm sorry. I will try to get you a goodie bag from Aslyn's mommy tomorrow. Okay?" I say with my best child-caring voice.

I stare at her a second as she nods silently with teary eyes.

"Look. I'm really sorry that you got mixed up in all this," I say with the most sympathetic tone I can muster. Whatever this is.

"Why were those people trying to take our picture?" she asks with child-like innocence.

I ponder the question for a minute. Paparazzi were a part of my life with Ashton—I expected them. But that's not my current reality—at least I don't think it is. Could this be about the Cannes event? Could it be something Jake did? What else could this be about?

"I'm not sure. Maybe it's because you are just so darn cute," I tease giving her a little tickle.

She snickers to herself.

I look back in the rear view mirror again for signs of paparazzi. I see one trailing close behind us. What are they doing? I stare for a moment and then I see another possible paparazzi car. Crap. How can I get us out of this?

"Look out!" Christina screams and points ahead, but I don't have the time to stop. I'm running right into—

Ouch. My head hurts. My body hurts. This is not good. I start my orientation process. Where am I? What happened? Who's tapping me? I see a blur. Christina is tapping me. I look down, I am covered in white power from the deployed air bag.

"Are you okay?" Christina asks shaking my right shoulder.

I open my eyes. "Um, yes, I think so." Then, realizing we wrecked, I quickly come to my senses, "Christina, are you ok? Why aren't you buckled?"

"I unbuckled after the crash. I'm fine, but I think you hit your head on this," she gestures to the center console.

There are siren lights all around us. Now, someone is running to the passenger side of the car. He's knocking on the window. It's Jake. What is he doing here?

"Christina, open the door!" Jake yells from outside the window.

She opens the door and they embrace. "Oh my beautiful girl! Are you okay?" He scans her body for injury.

"Yes. Daddy. I'm fine, but she's not," Christina replies pointing to my forehead.

"Oh, we'll get her all fixed up," he says hugging Christina even tighter.

"I don't know what I would do without you. I'm so glad you are okay," he tears up. I've never seen Jake so emotional in all my life. Maybe things have changed.

His eyes meet mine and finally he asks, "Are you okay?"

"Yes. I think so. A little shook up. I hit my head. I think it's bleeding." I pause and then say, "Who are you?" I pretend to have lost my memory. I am curious how he would react if I actually did lose my memory.

"It's me. Jake," he responds loudly and slowly as if I'm deaf.

I don't say a word. I see a handsome Emergency Medical Technician from the ambulance standing behind Jake waiting to check me.

"Don't move ma'am. I'm going to check things out and make sure you are ok" he says.

"Please do check me out," I flirt with the EMT.

He checks for signs of spinal injury, then shines a bright light in both my eyes, "Is it okay if I ask you a few questions?"

"Absolutely! Is one of them, 'Will you have dinner with me Friday night?'" I ask naughtily in ear shot of Jake.

"No, but I appreciate the offer," he respectfully declines. "Now, can you tell me what you remember?"

"Yes. The paparazzi were trailing us and I couldn't seem to get away," I reply truthfully.

"The paparazzi?"

"Yes. They were stalking us." I plead, "Look. I'm not crazy. Ask her." I point to Christina.

Jake frowns and looks at Christina. "What's paparazzi?" she asks.

"People who take pictures," Jake clarifies, and Christina nods in agreement.

"Why were they chasing you?" the EMT asks.

"I don't know—to get tabloid footage I suppose. Isn't that what they do?" I wearily state.

"I see," he responds politely.

"Ask her if she knows who I am?" Jake pipes in. And now they both think I'm delusional.

"Do you recognize this man?" he asks per Jake's request.

"Yes. Jake Green. I used to date him in college," I reply with one hundred percent honesty, waiting for him to lash back and say that he's my husband, but he doesn't.

"So, you do recognize me?" Jake says to me.

"Of course I do. I was just kidding. I'm fine," I drop my head back laughing hoping it will spark some joy in Jake's world.

"Ha. Ha." Jake responds sarcastically and focuses his attention back on Christina. "Sweetie, are you really okay? Do you have any bumps or scratches? The nice man checking Rachael can check you too," Jake asks Christina.

"I'm good," Christina says shaking her head.

After the EMT clears me, I'm approached by a police officer, "Madam, can I get your license and registration?"

I hand him my driver's license, and Jake pulls out the vehicle registration sheet from the glove box of the car and gives it to him.

"Can you tell me what happened?" he asks.

I repeat what I've just told the EMT. He listens carefully. I don't mention being chased. I simply just admit fault that I lost control of the wheel. He nods several times and finally he says, "Did you know your license is expired?"

"It is? I had no idea. I will get that taken care of right away," I reply.

That's really weird. It's not like me in any reality to ignore details like getting a driver's license renewed, I think as I put it back in my wallet.

A few minutes later the tow truck arrives to take the car for repair. Jake works out the details with the tow truck driver, while Christina and I wait in Jake's car. I watch him and I do my best to remember any details about our marriage hoping that this second wham to my head has knocked some sense back into it.

"Ready to roll?" Jake says as he gets in the car.

I nod preparing myself for my spanking.

"Well, I want to hear all about Aslyn's party. Did you have fun?" he asks Christina sweetly. He's such a good dad. I have to admit I admire that about him.

"Yes. I had so much fun. There was a moon bounce and cake and Suzie was there too." Christina shares with joy. "And I learned to do a flip!" she says as she lets out a big yawn along with a childlike giggle.

"Good I'm so glad you had fun," Jake replies to Christina as he turns on the radio. I look back and see Christina is falling asleep in her car seat. Her head is slumped to one side and she looks like a little angel.

I look to Jake and consider asking one of the million things on my mind, but instead I say, "Hey Jake, would it be okay if we could talk about a few things when we get home?"

"Absolutely, after Christina is in bed," he whispers as he gestures to Christina asleep in the back.

"Oh. Yes. Of course," I say shuffling in my seat. "Yes. When we are home," I whisper.

— Journal Entry —

I surrender. There's a big difference between being out of control by overreacting and going crazy and being out of control because you have surrendered to the conscious forces of nature.

Today, I was out of control because I over-reacted and it could have ended badly for me and Christina.

Now, I'm ready to surrender to being instead of to all these programs and systems keeping me trapped in the constructs of this reality. Where can I be free of these constructs?

13

What's True for Me?

WHEN WE ARRIVE HOME Jake seems calm and content despite the crazy afternoon. I watch him as he helps Christina get changed and ready for bed. I find her absolutely adorable with her wavy brunette hair in pigtails wearing her pink Cinderella night gown. She has never looked so endearing. She's a princess in so many ways. Jake carefully places her in her bed. And once she's settled she lets out a great big loud yawn and cuddles with her teddy bear. I look at Jake and smile feeling a warm, honey energy of gratitude run down my spine.

We make our way downstairs and into the living room. "Would you like a glass of wine?" Jake asks.

The word wine brings up, oh, so much, and my feelings of gratitude quickly changes into a wild rush of angst all through my body. I have no idea how he will react when I tell him I'm pregnant. And I have no idea how to tell him about the confrontation with Katie. What will he say? Do

I want to hear it? I give a startled jump as he waits for a response, "Yes. Please. Thanks." I finally say in denial of the positive pregnancy test.

He pulls a beautiful bottle of red wine from the minibar behind us and pours just a few ounces for me to taste. He hands me the glass and says, "Aside from the car accident, how was your day? You seemed very busy, did everything go well?"

"Jake, I had an incredible day. Pierre and I created this amazing shoe design today," I say as he hands me the glass. I take a sip, "Oh wow. This wine is amazing. What is it?" I ask handing the glass back for it to be filled.

"It's from our vineyard. Christina named it Flower," he replies as if he's trying to impress a guest.

"Oh. Yes, of course," I reply feeling as if I would know about the vineyard. I guess this would be a good time to tell him about my amnesia, pregnancy or the event with Katie. And then I can ask about the paparazzi.

"So, what do you want to talk about? What's on your mind?" he asks, handing me the filled glass.

"Okay. Well, here's the thing," I say, then taking a few large gulps of wine to calm my nerves.

"Yes," he replies as he surveys a series of email messages on his iPhone.

"Um. Well. I don't quite know where to start," I say looking at him, hoping to receive some sort of conscious connection.

"Rachael, just tell me. Jeez for once in your life just tell me the truth," he snaps and finally looks up from his iPhone.

"Fine. Well here's the thing," I reach again for the glass of wine.

"What?" He demands my response.

"I have amnesia and I'm pregnant," I just blurt it out and wait for his response or reaction.

He jumps up and takes the glass from my hand and gulps it down. "Jake?" I whine sweetly.

"Pregnant? You're pregnant. How do you know?" he asks.

"Well, I took a test," I say dumbly as I watch him pour his second glass of wine and gulp it down. "Jake!" I yell requesting his attention.

"Well, you know sometimes those tests are wrong," he nods a few times while shaking and pointing his wine glass at me.

I've never seen him so frazzled. He usually seems to have every moment contained with poise and confidence. This is a whole new side of Jake. I sort-of like it!

"Jake, I am pregnant. I know I am. I'm sick in the mornings. I can tell. It's not the end of the world. Geesh,." I say clearly as I watch him pace around the room for a few minutes. "Jake! Stop! What's really wrong?" I pause and after a moment ask, "Is it Katie? I know about you and her." I roll my eyes to the sky and take a deep breath.

I watch as his eyes meet mine, and for the first time I feel he really sees me.

"Kate? What do you know about Kate?" he asks.

"Really? Fine. I overheard someone say you and Katie were kissing in your office," I cross my arms and reply.

"Oh." he laughs nervously, "It's not like it seems, Rachael."

"Okay. I'm listening. How is it, Jake? Because it seemed pretty legit based on the information I heard and how Katie responded when I confronted her," I reply coolly. "You know, it's been a crappy few days, why don't you tell me what's really going on?" I state.

"Okay. Here's the truth, there's this crazy obsessed guy at the office. He's been all over Kate so when the time was right, we presented him with a kiss. You know, to get him off her tail. That's all. It was nothing. It's all pretend," he shrugs.

"Really?" I say in disbelief.

"Really. It was nothing. I was helping a friend—so to speak," he says clearly, thinking that I'm buying this story.

"Well if that's true, I acted like a complete jerk to her at the party. I was so rude to Katie," I reply.

"What do you mean? What happened?" Jake asks.

"I confronted her in front of the entire party. I accused her of lying and adultery," I pause thinking about our interaction. "Actually, come to think of it, she could have easily told me the truth. Why didn't she? What is her story? Who's Aslyn's dad? Is she in a relationship?" I ask.

He sits back and takes a deep sigh as if he's about to spill his guts, then seems to have second thoughts. "Why are you asking that? She's your best friend. Why are you asking me? Shouldn't you be asking her?"

"Jake!" I whined like I used to when we were dating. "I said it earlier. Did you hear me? I have amnesia. I must have. I don't remember our relationship." I reply with frustration.

He nods and waits for me to tell him more.

"Okay. Here goes. Remember that night in the hospital?" I take a breath and see his concerned stare. "Of course you do," I shake my head stupidly. "Erm, well, when I woke up I didn't remember my life with you. I've been pretending I remember our life this whole time—and I'm done pretending." I pause hoping he'll jump in and save me from the details.

"Okay," he replies and waits for my response.

"I didn't think you were my husband. I mean. I remember you from five years ago, but I don't remember getting married or Christina. Nothing. It was all blank. I knew I didn't want to stay in the hospital so I lied and said I was fine," I clasp my hand over my mouth.

"Okay. I'm listening," Jake replies.

"Pierre told me you knew. Why didn't you tell me?" I pout purposely to manipulate him to give me an honest and true response. At this point I think that's the only way he'll tell me anything.

"I thought you were okay. I kept asking you if you were okay. The doctors said you would recover from it quickly. I thought when you said you were okay—you were okay," he replies defensively.

"Oh," I say taken aback. I spare him the additional details. He's going to think I'm crazy if I tell him I thought I was married to Hollywood movie star and famous producer, Ashton Hunt. Could I have just filled the absence in my mind with my dream life with Ashton? Could that be an illusion?

He shifts uncomfortably and offers me a concerned look. Sometimes Jake is really hard to read. What is he thinking?

"Rachael, I'm sorry. I'm listening," he replies deliberately and genuinely.

I move to his side. Our hips and knees are now touching which makes me feel a bit uncomfortable, but necessary for us to become closer. I turn and take both of his hands in mine. I'm not one hundred percent sure if what about I'm to say will change anything, but I blurt it out anyway, "It's okay, Jake. I'm yours now. I'm ready to give this baby an incredible home and life with us." So, there I said it. And I meant it—and I secretly hope this is a bizarre dream that I will soon wake from.

"That's sweet," Jake replies.

"Sweet?" I reply with a question. Really? How can I possibly live a life with this man? A man that is so distant that he can't even receive a stronger more intimate relationship from his wife and new baby in his life.

"Look Rachael, I don't want to add to the chaos of this situation; however, we've planned to divorce. Your heart hasn't been with me for a long time," he says sheepishly.

I stare at him. My intuitive radar is on high alert. I know he's hiding something. Something isn't right, but I just can't put my finger on it. "Oh? I see. Is that why you have been so distant?" I probe for clarity. "Well, we can change that still right? Think about the new baby. I can't raise a child alone. I don't want to raise him or her alone. This baby deserves a father." I find myself fighting for my marriage. I can't help but see an image of Jake being a wishbone where Katie has one arm and I have the other.

"Look Rachael," he lifts my chin to bring my eyes to meet his, "I love you. You were my best friend—and our lives have gone separate ways. We just don't work anymore." I can sense him creating even more distance between us as he speaks.

"No. We can change this! Don't you want to change this?" I ask.

"Not anymore. We've tried. It's over." Jake replies.

"But I'm different now!" I scream. "Something has happened to me. The accident changed me. You can see that, right?"

He starts to nod and then shakes his head. "It doesn't matter now."

"Really? Jake, why not give it a try until after the baby is born? If it doesn't work out we can separate then. Are you willing to give it a go? Can we give it a go?" I plead. "Is it Katie? Is it someone else?"

"Rachael, why are you suddenly so determined to be with me? We haven't really been together in a long time. It's too late," he speaks coldly as if he's just delivering a line.

"What? It's not too late." I start to cry. I pick up the entire wine glass and consider throwing it across the room. "Look. I've lost my effing memory and a bunch of weird stuff is going on. I need someone on my side here." I drop my right cheek on his thigh and curl up in a fetal position next to him. He puts his hand on my shoulder and doesn't say a word. Finally, I roll on my back and look up to him as I used to when we were dating and say, "Well, do you want to watch a movie and forget about all this for this moment?"

"Yes. I would love to." He smiles and gently rubs my arm as he adds his famous line from college, "I'll make the popcorn. You pick the movie." Suddenly I feel like I'm back in the dorm with my best friend.

A few minutes later Jake returns and hands me a big bowl of popcorn for us to share. I chose *City of Synchronicity* Blu-Ray starring Ashton Hunt. I figure if I can't be with Ashton I might as well watch him.

We spend the rest of the evening cuddled up on the couch, eating popcorn, laughing together and watching some of Ashton's best work.

— Journal Entry —

Ah. It feels good to surrender to me. Telling Jake was intense, but now I don't have to spend so much energy holding back the thoughts, the stories, the possible outcomes. I feel incredibly vulnerable, yet at the same time I've never felt so free to be me. So in other words, when someone is back-stabbing and rude, I will express myself in a powerful way to get them to change.

Just to get my mind clear. I'm writing these words and their possible definitions:

1. ENERGY, CONSCIOUSNESS & SPACE: Are what you are & what you know is true.

2. KNOWER: When you know that you know that you know?

3. WHAT MOVES YOU? This is what turns you on – not desire.

4. FIRST STEP: Everything is new and has a sense of wonderment.

5. OPENNESS: You are the conscious space and can be all energies within that space.

6. LIBERATION: Beyond identity, judgment, definitive states, viewpoints will stop liberation and consciousness.

7. JUDGMENT: Seduction of identifying with good/bad and/or right/wrong

8. INQUIRY: That childlike wondering and curiosity.

9. CHOICE: Usually, you can choose from the mind which is right based on preconceived ideas; however, you can choose from the energy of what feels true from the Knower within you.

10. THREE SENSATIONAL AWARENESSES is connected embodiment of the head (know), heart (perceive), gut (receive, be)

11. ZERO VIEWPOINT: Unprocessed information is observed without judgment, rational thinking or emotional feeling and choice can be created from the zero point.

14

Possibility

IT'S BEEN FOUR WEEKS since my fall. I haven't uncovered or recovered any new information from my memory but I have given up on my delusion and illusion of being saved by my knight in shining armor—a.k.a. movie star Ashton Hunt.

I've also been curiously seeing things as they are instead of creating stories or judgment about them. I'm simply approaching each situation with what Pierre calls "zero viewpoint." Pierre explains it as how things are just what they are without judgment or story. And the cool thing is when you have zero viewpoint you become aware of the areas in your life where you are resisting, reacting and fighting other people's viewpoints, and where you create what he calls "polarity"—which ultimately leads to dis-ease and disease. I have to admit this way of being allows me to be in personal choice instead of feeling like a victim all the time.

Jake has consistently created separation and distance between us. I find myself writing the same things over and over in the dragon journal. For instance: Is Jake hiding something? What has he done? Why are Jake and Christina so cold to me? What have I done? And why won't they talk to me about it? What can I do or be to get them to open up? It really doesn't matter as I've been working from 7 a.m. to 11 p.m. daily to prepare for the Cannes trip—which is fantastic. I love designing and creating shoes. I now know why Ashton worked so many long hours. I get his desire to work and create. It is so much fun. And in my unique case, I also get to hide from Jake, Christina and this bizarre life I don't remember.

I walk into the office and find Gaby with a fruit roll-up on her forefinger. She has a wad in her mouth when she says, "How are ya, Rachael?"

Wow. She's actually in a joyous mood today. I'm shocked and have no idea how to respond. I wonder if her new boyfriend has had some impact? I saw them kissing last night in the parking lot on my way home.

"I'm fabulous. How are you?" I reply, not completely expecting a positive response.

"I'm fabulous too! How's the Henderson project coming along?" she asks thoughtfully.

"Oh. They've sent me the criteria. I'm finishing the sketches today," I say with a smile.

"Nice. Can I see what you've come up with so far?" Gaby asks curiously.

I reach into my briefcase and hand her my two new sketches.

"Hi beautiful," Pierre surprises me from behind me and

kisses me on the nape of my neck. This sends shivers down my spine. I absolutely love the affection Pierre expresses. It's clear that it's just presented in kindness and doesn't mean anything. I'm enjoying it so much—and definitely not making it into anything that it is not.

"Hi, Pierre. Gaby is looking over the new Henderson sketches. I'd love to see what you think, too."

Now they are both reviewing the sketches. After the longest moment Gaby says, "This is good. Really good, Rachael. Although I would change the buckle. It's some of your best work."

"It's more than good. It's absolutely fantastic! Great job, Rachael. And I personally love the buckle," Pierre responds.

"Thank you," I gratefully reply.

"Rachael, can I talk to you a minute?" Pierre asks.

"Absolutely," I respond following him to his office.

"Rachael, I'm worried about you," Pierre looks genuinely concerned.

"You are? I'm fabulous. Thanks to you and how you've facilitated change for me," I smile.

"Look. You are coming up with these incredible designs—better than I have ever seen, but I feel you aren't really living! You have been here until eleven or midnight every night this week. I know these designs aren't taking you that long. What's really going on?"

"Um," I look down.

"What is it?" he asks.

"Well, I guess, I would rather be here than anywhere else. I'm having fun creating," I say quite plainly.

"Well, that's totally your choice. Could there be something you are hiding from?" he asks.

"Yes. Jake." I reply knowing he already knows I'm avoiding the intimacy of life and especially in my relationship with Jake.

He nods in acknowledgment. "Well, I did something for you. I purchased an entire day for you at the spa." He hands me an envelope with a gift certificate stamped with today's date.

I stare at it. "No. I can't go to the spa today. We have to get ready for the charity ball for Stiletto Stampede and for the Cannes trip. I have a ton to do. A ton," I protest.

"You can't go or you won't choose it? Honey, everything is ready for the charity ball tomorrow night, and we have plenty of time to get everything ready for the Cannes trip. Okay? Can you make a different choice now?" Pierre asks in a way where I can really see that I often feel I don't have a choice.

"Totally. Yikes. I'm changing that right now," I nod. "Yes, the spa! Let's go!"

"They open in an hour. Our appointments are already booked," he says with a wink.

"Are you going with me?" I ask excitedly as I find myself totally turned on with the thought of spending a spa day with Pierre.

"Yes, of course. I couldn't let you have all the fun," he laughs.

"Mmmm. I guess I can have some fun with you," I say flirting back with him. And then I start to backpedal when I realize I'm flirting with my business partner, and he may not appreciate the unprofessional nature of it. I giggle, "Well, you know what I mean," I purposefully say with a bashful nature.

∗ ∗ ∗

As we enter the spa my mobile rings. I dig through my Michael Kors bag and when I find it the caller has hung up. Darn. I stare at the display. Private caller. Private caller? Who is that? Over the past few weeks I've discovered I have very few friends. In fact, Jake, Pierre, Gaby, and Lucy are the only calls I believe I have received since my fall. It makes me wonder if I have friends. It seems that someone would care enough to call if they had heard I was in the hospital. Hmmm. Maybe I don't have any friends? Maybe it's all about work?

"Miss, we don't allow cell phones," barks the indignant woman from the spa's front desk.

"No problem, they just hung up," I say politely to get her off my back. I frown at the phone waiting for the message light to show up. "Is everything okay?" Pierre asks.

I nod and see the woman giving me a deep evil stare.

"Wow. If looks could kill, she would be killing all their clients," Pierre whispers jokingly about her phone judgment.

I laugh still wondering about the caller. I wonder if it was a doctor that could offer some insight about my memory.

A few minutes later, the front desk lady pops her head out from under her paperwork and says, "Miss. It's your turn. Please place your personal items in the basket." She holds out a basket and waits for me to place my purse and other personal items in it.

I do as I'm told. I was hoping Pierre would join me, but he gives a nod for me to go ahead. When I'm about to drop my purse in the basket I hear the voicemail tone and I just can't wait. So when the receptionist isn't looking I grab my phone and slip it in my pocket.

"Thanks for calling Salon 11:11, can you please hold," I hear her response to her phone caller. When she looks up, I become Obi Wan Kenobi from Star Wars and ask her to drop all thoughts in her head about my rule invasion: Everything is fine. Continue as normal. Move along. Move along.

"Hi. I'm ready," I state joyously.

"Okay, follow me." I follow as she takes me down a short corridor and opens the door to a beautifully-lit massage room.

As she opens the door, a gorgeous twenty year-old blond introduces herself. "Hi Rachael, I'm Janie, I'll be taking care of you today. We're going to start with your body wrap. Then, we'll do your pedicure and we'll end with your facial and hair styling. Do you have any questions for me before we get started?"

I'm about to ask if we can arrange to some of my spa sessions with Pierre, but instead I simply ask, "Um. How long do you think this all will take?"

"Maybe four or five hours. We'll definitely be done by five." Janie replies with a friendly, joyous smile.

"Would it be possible for me to return one phone call

before we start? It'll just take one minute," I ask politely ready to reach for my phone.

"Salon 11:11 is a place for you to relax. That's why we remove all personal and electronic items before we begin. We believe they are both addictive and obsessive. The answer is no. You can leave and make your phone call or you can stay for your treatments," Janie replies.

"Okay," I reply in defeat. I feel this combative nature coming out of this beautiful girl that makes me want to fight.

"Okay. Please remove your clothes and lie down under the sheet," she gestures to the massage table. "I'll be back in a couple minutes," she says as she walks out the door.

"Okay," I reply. I respond knowing it will be a least three minutes before she returns—which is just enough time for me to listen to the voice message and send a text response if necessary.

I quickly strip down and jump under the sheet on the massage table. As soon as I'm settled under the sheet, I press the voice mail button and place it to my ear. The message starts with "I'm pleased to inform you," but before I hear another word there's a rap on the door. Damn. I quickly tuck my mobile under my belly before I'm caught.

"Ready?" Janie asks gleefully.

"Yes, of course," I say praying no one will text or call while my phone is under my belly for the next hour during my massage.

Janie starts my massage at my upper back and after a few minutes I feel my phone buzz and vibrate.

"What was that?" Janie asks not yet suspecting anything.

"Um. Oh," I sigh, "I don't know."

She continues to rub my shoulders with hesitation when my phone vibrates again. Damn it.

"There it is again. What is that?" She asks.

"Oh that. It's my sex toy," I say.

She doesn't say a word, but I can tell she's uncomfortable. Ping—I hear the text message alert—this is a noisy sex toy.

"Do you have a phone?" she says seeming slightly offended.

"Um. No. I make that noise sometimes," I say as the phone pings again. Damn it. "And I'm reaching an intimate moment now and—oh—I." I start to make some sounds and then realize it's not doing any good, so instead I confess. "Okay, fine. Yes, I have a phone."

"Please hand it over." she says slowly and waits for me to place the phone in her overly-lubricated hands.

"Fine," I reluctantly concede.

"Thank you. This will be with your other things when you check out. Now, let's continue," she says very professionally.

I lay still and try to relax, but I can't stop my thoughts of intimacy with Pierre and the phone message. It's like being on a merry-go-round, and it sounds something like this: I wonder what Pierre thinks about me. Was this spa day meant for us to spend the day together? Or maybe he just deeply cares for everyone and I'm nothing special. I wonder who called. What were they pleased to tell me? Maybe I won something? Maybe it was my true identity—or maybe not.

When my massage is complete, my head is so twisted

151

that I don't know what to do with myself. I arrive in the next room with four occupied pedicure chairs. I scan the room hoping to see Pierre, but he is nowhere to be found. I sigh loudly in dismay.

I'm greeted by another lady in a black smock, "Pick a color and please have a seat." She says pointing at the large display of nail polishes, "I'll just be a moment."

I sit next to a woman reading a magazine. Without looking at me she says, "Wow. That was a big sigh for a woman at the spa. Are you okay?"

"Oh. I'm fine. I was just hoping to see someone," I say and I let out another deep sigh.

"Wow. You should have been in here ten minutes ago. The shoe artist Pierre Brock was in here getting a pedicure. The whole room was roaring. He's hilarious!" she says.

"Oh," I reply trying to hide my disappointment.

She continues to mindlessly flip through her magazine as she launches into a story about how she hasn't had a pedicure in over a year because of money and blah, blah, blah. I don't hear much of the story because my head is one hundred percent in fantasy about Pierre. When she continues with how terrible her life has been this past year, I nod and act as if I heard every word.

A moment later, she looks up at me and says, "Oh my! You look really familiar. Do I know you?"

"I don't think so?" I respond in shock as I have no idea who she is—but then again I have no idea who I am either. "Where do you believe we have met?"

"Oh. I don't know where we've met. My name is Sharon

Parker," She reaches out her hand. As our hands meet she gasps, "Wait, you're Rachael, aren't you?"

I nod to Sharon as my pedicurist gestures to a newly emptied chair, "It's your turn," she demands. There's a lot of demanding in this spa. I'm actually surprised Pierre recommends this place. I mean he's so easy going and this whole bossy-worker thing is not exactly relaxing. I'm just saying.

I sit in my pedicure chair hoping to get a chance to talk more with Sharon, but she is soon thereafter shuffled off to another room. I wonder how she knows me? Maybe I could start screaming her name as I run through the spa? That would make this control freakish spa go nuts. I can see the headlines now: Crazy Woman with Sex Phone Massager Kicked out of Spa—Could be Dangerous! Dang, the thought of the paparazzi hearing any of this makes my stomach knot. Yikes! Okay, mind, stop! Stop this craziness!

I never do see Sharon after that. After my final treatment I arrive in the waiting room and find Pierre there flipping through a Men's Health magazine. He looks up at me with warm eyes, "Wow. You look beautiful. Are you feeling rejuvenated and ready for our next adventure?"

"Thank you! Absolutely, I'm ready for adventure now!" I respond with a curtsy.

"Did you just curtsy?" Pierre smirks.

"I did," I reply with a giddy laugh.

"Do you want to grab a bite?" he holds out his hand for me to take it.

"Yes, that would be fantastic," I reply as I slowly take his hand and we leave together.

Once we are seated in his car, Pierre checks his phone display and suddenly I realize I've completely forgotten about the voicemail. I press the voicemail button and brace myself. I listen carefully. It's an attorney from Jake's office. He says he's pleased to inform me that our divorce papers will arrive via Fed-Ex tomorrow. He sounds like a total robot almost as if he's reading a script.

As I watch Pierre responding to his text messages, I think about how I've changed since we've met and how I've changed since I realized I was married to Jake. After everything that has happened, true and not true, there is a part of me that wants to hold on to some identity and something that I remember, and that is Jake. I have to admit I sort of like the idea being a wife and a mother. I gaze at the diamond on my finger—the one thing that has been a permanent fixture since I found it in that hospital bag. I pull the ring off and place it in my purse with a twinge of sadness and regret.

A moment later Pierre starts the car and we are on the way to the restaurant, "Are you okay?" Pierre asks, knowing that something has gotten me down since the spa.

"Oh, that was about our divorce," I say in dismay.

"I had heard something about that from Jake. He told me how much he dearly loved you, and how the marriage just wasn't working," Pierre replies.

"Oh, I see." I say feeling somewhat disconnected from everything.

— Journal Entry —

Breathe. I take a breath and take in all these sensations of joy and bliss.

Alright - here's what I'm aware of and what I'm choosing now :)

1. Pierre and I are creating a massive inspirational impact and message for those ready to live: "What moves you? Take your first steps with us!"

2. Jake and I are not meant to be together. NO!

3. And I sense something uber awesome changing with these inner feelings about Ashton Hunt. Maybe that was a previous life thing? Or maybe I've watched too many movies—either way I'm going to do what I can to meet him. Not as a stalker, but I can find a way. Um. Yeah. Maybe a shoe design or something...

15

Acknowledgment

IT'S EXACTLY NINE-THIRTY LA time when we arrive at the charity ball for Stiletto Stampede®. This is Sinder Ella Soles first official charity event, and I am so excited that we can support this great organization raising funds to fight cancer. As I enter the ballroom, I can feel Pierre's eyes on me. I secretly love the admiration. I sit in the reserved seating, cross my legs and gaze at him with my inner Mona Lisa smile.

"You look beautiful," he whispers in my ear as his face breaks into a true, affectionate smile.

"Why thank you kind sir," I say with my best Southern Belle accent. As I say it I notice that I'm finally sensing the essence of joy in my world. I'm not sure if this change in inner state has to do with the grand divorce finale, or Pierre and I creating a closer connection, or maybe it's from my choice to give up the illusion of Ashton Hunt, but whatever it is I'm so grateful to be joyful again!

"Would you like to dance?" Pierre asks as he takes my hand.

"Yes, Thank you," I giggle.

Pierre starts our dance with a confident powerful twirl.

"Wow. You really got into the swing of things," I joke. I know he's a skilled dancer after years of dancing with Ashton. When Ashton and I dance we effortlessly impress the crowd because Ashton knows his stuff.

"When I first learned the jitterbug I sprained my ankle," I laugh. "Ashton carried me home five blocks and babied me for the next five days," I say accidentally, hoping Pierre won't ask too many questions about Ashton. Oh, wait. Did that really happen or is that the delusional memory?

"Ashton? Was Ashton your boyfriend before Jake?" he asks.

"Yeah. Funny that I remember that," I say lightheartedly. Damn. How would I know that, and how would I know how to dance if I didn't learn it from Ashton? Jake can't dance at all. Would I even have had reasons to take lessons? Oh, stop brain—not now—everything is happy now. Okay, just be present. Breathe. Breathe. Breathe.

"I had to learn how the feet move so I could make better shoes," Pierre says with a wink.

"Oh really?" I say as he lifts me over his shoulders and swings me under his legs and back up.

"Wow. You're an incredible dancer," I laugh. I'm about to add "even better than Ashton," but instead follow-up with, "You've really made this event special for everyone."

"No. *We've* made this event incredible. You really took

the lead on this one. I am grateful to have you on my team," he looks directly into my eyes with a deep presence.

"Awww. Thank you. I'm grateful for you too," I respond with a confident smile.

"Rachael, you are like the sun. You are more powerful than you could ever know. You're truly a force of nature. You give everything life and joy. That's what you are. And I'm so grateful to have the opportunity to work with you."

"Oh, come on," I respond, uncomfortably denying his comment. Then after a breath I receive his beautiful acknowledgment. "Hey, let's mingle," I say changing the topic.

"No, let's not. I'm not much of the mingling type. Our shoes were meant for dancing." He grabs my hand and twirls me into his chest once again.

"So, you think I'm a force of nature?" I laugh feeling more like I'm in a dream than ever before. I have adored Pierre since the first time I saw his designs. This is very awesome and surreal. It's like a dream come true.

"Let's just say I think you are pretty different," he replies.

"You do?"

"I do," he smiles and kisses my hand.

The song ends and the master of ceremonies asks everyone to return to our tables. He starts with a series of thank-yous including Brock's Blissful Soles and Sinder Ella Soles. Then the MC continues by saying, "It's time to give the giant check to Stiletto Stampede." Suddenly I'm not listening to a word he's saying. I'm watching Pierre write a note on his cocktail napkin. I am doing my best to read every word. It reads, "I'm leaving for France tomorrow. I care for you. I have something I need to tell you about Jake, but we can't talk now." After I read the note he rips it up and puts it in his empty water glass. What? Why would a guy that has opened the doors for me to be more and receive more through oneness tell me we can't talk now? I've been with him for weeks, why would he spring this on me now?

"I can't finish everything up on my own," I whisper wanting him to give me more.

"Yes. Yes, you can. Just ask questions and following what feels light. You can do whatever you desire. You are one potent being, my beautiful friend, like the sun." He gives me a big smile.

I respond with a little sad puppy dog face. "I'm going to miss you," I say with a deliberate pout.

"You'll be fine. You don't need me. I'll see you in France, and when you get there I'll tell you more—when others aren't around." He trails off and looks around the room.

I frown wondering if this is a test to keep me in question.

"I need to tell you something," Pierre says clearly.

"Oh yeah. Do I have to wait?" I ask jokingly kicking him under the table like a child.

"Yes. You do," he responds seriously and sweetly.

"Actually, Pierre, can we talk now—before you leave? I have something I need to tell you too. I don't think it can wait." I ramble timidly. I will use the pregnancy as the "something," but it's really my manipulative strategy to hear what's on his mind.

"Okay, let's get out of here. I'm not the socialite as you know," Pierre says matter-of-factly.

Somehow we make it to his house. We've been flirting with subtle gestures the entire taxi ride over. Well, at least I've been flirting, and it seems he is flirting back. My heart is pounding, butterflies are fluttering in my stomach, and it feels as if I'm cheating on Ashton or Jake. I watch as Pierre reaches for the doorknob. A nervousness starts to bubble up now that I am going to tell him about the baby. This is it. My chest feels as if it's going to explode.

As he opens the door I hear, "Hi Dad." It's Gaby. She's sitting at his kitchen table with a laptop. "I'm planning the budget for the Cannes trip," she announces joyfully. I think I'm going to have a heart attack now.

"Here?" Pierre asks in confusion.

"Well, you know, Lucy has a date over, and we have no food in the house, again—so I came over." She rambles as she takes another bite of her leftover lasagna. "Hi Rachael. What are you guys working on tonight?" she asks with a mouthful of food.

"Oh. I was just, erm, picking up some—" I trail off and look for Pierre to complete my thought.

"Right. Rachael needed to pick up a few things I had here," Pierre replies with ease.

"Oh. I could have taken that to the office tomorrow," Gaby replies as Pierre walks towards one of the back rooms.

"Well, you could have, but we didn't know you would be here. Did we?" Pierre comments back to Gaby with a similar snotty adolescent attitude.

We reach the back bedroom and Pierre hands me a

portfolio. "Just take this. It's my collection of ideas. It'll give you some inspiration."

"Okay." I whisper and look down. "When can we talk?" I ask timidly.

"Look at me." I look up from the ground. "You've got what it takes to run Sinder Ella. Don't be scared. Follow the energy and make your choices based on the energy. And call me if you need anything specific. Okay?"

"Okay, but it's not about that." I start to leave and then I abruptly turn back to Pierre. "Pierre, I have something personal that I need to tell you," I say with my deepest inner potency.

"Sit." He closes the bedroom door and taps the chair next to the bed.

"Pierre, I want to tell you something. I've been waiting because I'm still not sure what storyline to follow and what has really happened regarding this." I shake my head down in some sort of denial.

"Okay, the story? Haven't we talked about this? Stories are just stories and they limit us in so many ways. So, what's the story that you are using here that may be limiting you?"

"Yes I get it. Totally, but you don't understand. This past action and choice has changed something in my timeline," I snicker.

Before he responds there's a rap on the front door. He looks at me as if to say wait.

"It's mom," Gaby yells from the kitchen.

We can hear Gaby talking with her on the other side of the door. I whisper as I stand, "Are you *married*?"

"No. Not exactly. Sit," he demands in honesty as he kisses my forehead. "I'm sorry about this."

"Not exactly?" I reply.

"We've been apart for five years, but have never filed for divorce. I've never had a reason to," he smiles warmly. We can hear Gaby and her mom getting closer to the door. "Can I call you once this craziness with Gaby and Kristin is over?"

"Ah. Yes. Okay." I say in hesitation as I uncomfortably walk past Gaby and her mom.

I walk slowly towards the waiting taxi hoping Pierre will run out and declare his love for me. I wonder for a moment why I am choosing him to be my knight in shining armor and why I always want some guy to be that knight. I know I don't need him to save me, or for him to save me from Jake and this crazy unknown land. I know I would like to just be with him more. With this awareness I choose to be real and live in ease. I take a deep breath and fill my body with energies of playful joy and sexy shoes.

— Journal Entry —

Pierre once said that you can choose the energy you are no matter what's going on outside you. And I looked at him and asked what the heck does that mean?

So he asked me—well—
Is an emotion an energy?

Is a thought an energy?
Is a feeling an energy?

And then he looked at me in a way and asked if that expression is an energy? And it's clearly not just a facial expression, it's an energy he transmits. It's beyond words. It just is what it is. And suddenly I acknowledge I am it too. He is controlling a state of being, and I'm being entrained to that state. How cool is that?

I'm giving up the attachment to the fantasy of Ashton. Instead, I'm choosing to be connected to him within the deep connectedness of conscious oneness! I know that sounds significant, but the truth of the matter is I can connect with anyone at any time through the energy of harmonic oneness.

16

Flow

WHEN I RETURN HOME I am bursting with these amazing sensations of joy mixed with ease and presence. I'm simply real. I know it's beyond the playful flirting with Pierre; it's simply the fact that I can just be me around Pierre, whoever I am. Now that I'm here, I'm excited to talk to Jake. Despite the divorce, Jake has become someone I can confide in. He has become that friend that really understands me. He's letting me stay at his house until I figure out a housing plan—not that I've had much time to think about it with the hours I'm putting in at Sinder Ella. I had never thought this was possible, but Jake and I have really had a breakthrough these past couple of weeks. I feel we can talk about anything now. In the last four weeks we've talked about everything under the sun, including my complete and utter mental confusion about my amnesia and pregnancy.

When I open the door I immediately hear lively sounds of children giggling and voices coming from the living room. I tiptoe around the corner and see Katie and Jake sharing a bottle of wine while Christina and Aslyn playing with Barbie dolls on the carpet. I see legal documents and papers scattered all over the coffee table.

"That's a cool pink convertible," I playfully say to the little girls.

"Hi Mommy," responds Christina as she continues to play.

"Hi!" I wave to Jake.

"I thought you'd be longer at your business function," he says as he stands and offers me a hug.

"I thought so too. I'll tell you about it later," I say to Jake feeling slightly awkward.

I look at Katie and she smiles. I gesture back politely with a little wave.

"Well, I'm off to bed," I fake a yawn and a big stretch while looking Jake in the eyes hoping he'll get the message that I would like him to be with me.

"Okay. Goodnight," he responds absently looking at the papers on the table.

I am very present as I walk down the hall and up the stairs to the bedroom. Despite feeling a little let down by both Jake and Pierre, I feel so grateful for everything. My body and being are humming with this beautiful conscious awareness that I haven't felt in years. It's fabulous to have my body buzzing with joy.

I step into my closet and notice for the first time since my fall I have this sense of gratitude for my life as it is. I slowly unbuckle my right sandal, slip it off and then do the same with the left. I unzip the back of my dress and allow it to drop to the ground. I stand there naked and take in whatever I can receive. Every little molecule in my body is on fire. Then with great joy I launch my body chest first on the bed, and as I land and let out a full body joyous stretch. I take a deep breath and decide it's time to journal. And with that I open the top drawer to the bedside table.

I gasp. It's not there. I toss my hand in and around the drawer for a minute and then physically put my head in the drawer. It's not there. My dragon journal is gone. Shit. I know I put it there last night.

Okay, Rachael, focus. What questions can I ask here to gain other awareness about the journal? Where is it? I look under the bed, in the bathroom and all over the room. What did I do with it? Does Jake have it? Okay, this isn't really helping in this situation as I'm getting a little stressed out, and now my OCD mental obsession stuff is bursting in full force. I try to remember every word I wrote about Jake, Christina, Katie, Pierre and Ashton. I know there were many unpleasant and angry sentences written. Augh. I specifically remember some very harsh words written about Jake that in many cases I regret and no longer mean. What do I do? Should I ask him?

Then suddenly I stop my obsessive head and I see the portfolio from Pierre. I start to thumb through the designs and next thing I know I find myself drawing something totally different and new.

A few hours later I place the sketch on the foot of the bed and slide under the covers. And just before I fall asleep

I hear that damn clanking again. I haven't heard it in a few weeks, but for some reason this time it doesn't even bother me. Maybe it's the A/C unit or something like that? Oh, well.

* * *

I wake the next morning and ask consciousness through my being to help me remain focused on bringing the best designs to Cannes. There is definitely this heaviness inside with the missing journal even though Jake didn't mention it and acted completely normal. We have come so far in our friendship, I don't want him to read something that might hurt him. I know if he reads all my private thoughts it will.

When I reach my office I'm starting to feel joyous once again. I look at my watch thinking Pierre is probably at the airport, and I wonder if I will hear from him before he leaves the country. I want to tell him about the design I came up with last night, inspired by his portfolio. Maybe I should call and tell him that we now have forty designs. Thirty-nine of them are all boxed up and ready for their voyage to France and my last one will travel with me. I peer at the boxes for a moment and feel an overwhelming sense of joy and gratitude. I'm calling Pierre. Why not? What if I just wish him good travels? Yes. I'm calling now.

Dang. He didn't answer. Okay. Time to clean this insanely messy office. I take a deep breath and turn on the radio to inspire my office cleaning task. I joyously dance as I organize contracts, printed emails and secretly hope the journal will magically appear under all these sketches and papers.

As I buzz around my office I hear Ashton's voice. I

look around the room wondering if I am hallucinating. Finally, my eyes land on the radio and I realize his voice is broadcasting from it. He's being interviewed. My heart leaps over and over again. Suddenly, my happy go-lucky cleaning buzz turns into a distraught AUGH. What is it with this guy? I want to be with him! And in some way I feel as if I'm supposed to be with him. So, I ask some questions to see if I can gain some awareness about this emotional junk. What is this? Well, it's a bizarre fantasy in my mind. Maybe it's from a past life or maybe it doesn't matter. Can I change this? Yes. How? Let it go.

Ahhh—with that I resolve to release this fantasy once and for all. I resolve that I've seen too many Ashton Hunt movies and when I was in the hospital I must have dreamt about it. I listen in for a minute as he talks about Fiji and the film. He talks about his new found freedom without technology, but not a word about any missing wife. I change the station and let it go. I know, now, my fantasy marriage with Ashton Hunt is simply an illusion from the past. There is no regret. I love my life as it is. I love me.

17

The Turn On?

FRANCE HERE I COME. I am staring at five Louis Vuitton suitcases. Two are filled with various gowns and two are filled with shoes I'll be wearing including the newest pair that I designed for Pierre from his portfolio, fresh from production. The last bag sits empty with its mouth open staring at me. I mean if I were home it would be filled with all kinds of beautiful clothes. I know exactly what I would take. Except I'm not there, I'm here, and I just let go of the thought that my old home ever existed. Time to let go of that again.

Okay, don't panic. I stare at my clothing possibilities. It's simply a matter of staying calm and choosing the best. I mean, just how hard can this possibly be? I obviously chose these clothes at one time or another. Why? I'm not so sure, but I did.

I sigh and survey the three possible outfits I've selected. I drop them on the bed and let out a deep sigh.

"Everything okay?" Jake startles me, and I look up with a jolt. He's standing in front of me wearing a six piece suit and Brock Soles. He looks good. "What are you doing?" He surveys the bed.

"Oh. Just packing," I sigh again loudly.

"Oh right, for Cannes," he says vaguely as he slips his shoes off and places them on his side of the closet. I watch as he drops his trousers and places them in a dry cleaning bag. Jake does this every evening after work. No surprises in the life with Jake Green. That man is a creature of habit. "Why the deep sigh?" he asks.

"I don't have anything appropriate to wear in France." I choose my words wisely and state the definitive awareness.

"What about this?" he pulls the black Eye Candy dress from the bed.

"Well, don't you think I need an elite name brand? I mean, this is nice, but it's not Reese Witherspoon nice," I sigh.

"What's 'Reese Witherspoon nice'?" he asks curiously.

"You know. It wouldn't be something a movie star would wear," I sigh yet again.

He looks at me and doesn't reply. I watch as he walks over to the dresser, picks up his wallet and opens it. Then he hands me his Black American Express charge card.

"What?" I ask in confusion.

"You leave in the morning. That gives you three solid hours of shopping. The limit is somewhere around five hundred thousand, I believe. So, go, have fun," Jake smiles.

I take the card and flip it around in my hand for a moment as he puts on a pair of shorts.

"Five hundred thousand? I don't think I need that much for clothes," I laugh.

"Well, you never know," he responds with a warm smile.

I smile in a way to let him know I'm very grateful.

An hour later as I'm walking through the doors of Neiman Marcus all my senses come alive. I smell the aromas in the air, see the beautiful clothing brands, and feel the energy of shopping. I feel like Cinderella seeing her gown and glass slippers for the first time. And the best part is I feel free. Free to be me. Free to choose, free to be in bliss—just plain free to be all of me, and it's not just because I'm shopping.

I take the escalator to the second floor and slowly walk down the corridor touching, feeling and taking in everything. Everything is beautiful inside and outside of me—the clothes, the shoes, the jewelry, the accessories and the pure sweet nectar of these creations. Everything is a turn on.

Okay, focus, clothes for Cannes. Hmm—what question can I ask here? What attire would be the greatest contribution to me and this event? I run my hand down a pair of red velvet pants.

"Those would look gorgeous on you." I'm startled by a voice and look up to see a twenty-something girl with straightened long blond hair and pouty lips in a designer black suit smiling at me. "Would you like to try them on?" she asks.

"Yes, please," I pull a size four from the rack and hand it to her.

I watch as she pulls a size two. "Just in case," she replies with a cute smile.

"I'm one of our trained personal shoppers. Would you like me to help you with your ensemble this afternoon?" she asks with great pride.

"Yes, absolutely! I'm looking for a few key professional pieces for the Cannes Fashion Festival in France," I say thoughtfully.

She takes me to a suite of dressing rooms. "My name is Kathryn. Can I get you some water or champagne?"

"Champagne would be great," I respond eagerly.

"Okay. Make yourself comfortable, and I'll be back in a few minutes," Kathryn replies.

When she returns, she hands me a glass of champagne and says, "I have chosen several selections for you." I watch as she rolls up a rack with a dozen professional suits. "See what you think about these?"

"Wow! These look fantastic. How could it get even better?" I say with great joy and excitement.

She stands back and gives my body a once over. Then she asks, "Hmm—D&G? Do you like D&G? That might make it even better," she responds with a smile.

"Yes! And Elie Tahari," I reply.

"Really? I think you'll want something that makes a greater statement than Tahari. Donna Karan has a new modern icon collection. I'll select a few suits from that collection as well. Okay?"

"That's great," I reply.

She rushes off and I take a swig of champagne. I touch,

feel and breathe in all the assorted outfits. Finally, I choose to try on the outfit with the hot red velvet pants.

A few minutes later Kathryn returns with another five iconic pant suits. I look at each one individually to see how well they will show off my footwear creations. I try on a few other suits and give a little twirl in the mirror. This makes me once again think about Ashton. He used to love to twirl me—or at least that's what I remember.

I continue to try on the others selections. Yes, yes, yes, and yes. It's like a little fabric orgasm and a total turn on!

I look at the price tags on each item—they range from $1,500 to $4,000 a piece—and I have a moment's pause. Ashton had resistance to spending over five thousand at a time. I look at the dresses and remember Jake's response about whatever it takes. And why do I care. I mean this might be the last time multi-millionaire Jake Green is buying. I look to Kathryn holding all five of my selections, which include over twelve items with tops, bottoms, jackets and accessories. "This is what you want?" she asks.

I take a breath, "Yes, absolutely."

She rings it up and I hand her the charge card. I don't even hear the amount.

"I'll have someone help you with these," she gestures to the five very large garment bags.

"Awesome! How could it get better?" I say again, more as a statement, but she takes it as a question.

"Well, we can also give you a VIP Platinum Personal Shopper card, which gives you a personal shopping experience each month at no charge. Would you be interested?"

"Yes. Absolutely," I respond in delight.

She gives me this beautiful card. I admire it for a moment and place it in my wallet as the bellboy arrives behind me with my garment bags on a dolly.

"Ready?" the bell boy asks.

"Oh, yes, absolutely," I reply.

After all the bags are settled in my car, I sit there tingling with exuberant joy.

18

Harmonic Oneness or Not

I'M HERE! I'M HERE! I've made it. Pierre has booked a stretch limo. When the driver opens the door, I see Pierre holding a flute of champagne for me. There is warm joyous music playing in the background. Pierre looks fabulous wearing linen trousers with a white linen button down top and a pair of tan Blissful Soles. "Hi love," he says warmly.

"Hi. Yay. I'm so excited!" I say as I plop in the seat next to him.

He smiles and then with a quiet secretive whisper says, "You're so silly."

"Whoa. So excited," I playfully jab him with my left elbow.

The front door opens, and the driver announces, "Looks like we are ready. Bags are in the back."

"Thanks, Jerry," Pierre nods.

I gaze out the window. The view is spectacular. There fields of plantations merging with the clear blue sky, and at this moment my being is merging in oneness with the beauty.

Despite the upcoming event, I feel calm knowing Pierre is the partner by my side. There is this awesome harmonic oneness between us. I've changed so much over the past few weeks. My entire world has shifted inside and out. I am beginning to really know who I am without my past story. I no longer obsess about what others do or say in regards to me as I know it's simply their view point. And I rarely make up or buy stories and assumptions about what others may be thinking or saying about me. Ha. The stories and fantasies of Ashton and Pierre don't count. So, there. I'm a completely different person. Look at me. I am joyous, happy and paparazzi-free. My old Hollywood friends wouldn't recognize me!

Even now thinking about my old life with Ashton, I mean, I miss what I thought I had with him, but it doesn't affect my state of being. I look at it as just another story or illusion from my past. I contemplate this thought for a moment. Now, looking back, I wonder if I created this illusion about Ashton to show me I didn't need to identify with anyone or any reality. Honestly, my current reality is quite delightful, and I don't need to hold on to that story. My life right now is fun and joyous—probably more joyous than ever before. Look at my life now. I'm a famous footwear designer, which I've always wanted to be. I'm pregnant and becoming a mother, which is fabulous. I am already a mother to this amazing little girl. And to top it off, I can hardly believe I am in Cannes waiting for the world to see our designs. My company's designs! I see a vision in my mind of my Sinder Ella sandals headlining every major fashion magazine in the world, and it brings tingles all over my body. It's really a dream come true.

"Can you believe Sinder Ella Soles is going to be in the spotlight in just a few hours?" I ask Pierre.

"Of course they are! We are creators!" Pierre uncrosses his legs and now we are knee to knee. He takes my hands in both of his. "There is something that I need to tell you, Rachael."

A jolt of adrenaline flies through my body. This is it? "Were you waiting for a perfect time?" I ask offering up my cute-eye-stare.

"I didn't want to stir things up, but you have to know," he trails off as the driver stops at our destination.

Out the window, we see Lucy running enthusiastically towards the limo. "I'm sorry, it's going to have a wait." He snickers, "I thought this was a longer trip."

I feel a slight flush come to my cheeks. "Pierre, ask me. Tell me. Just tell me quickly," I demand urgently, not wanting Lucy to be a part of this magical moment—thinking this has to be about our past or future relationship.

"They're starting! They're starting!" Lucy is yelling from outside the limo. "Come on!" she motions.

Ohmigod. Here we go. I feel a sudden leap of exhilaration. I quickly scoop up my personal bags from the driver.

"I'm going to run on down there. Can you get this settled?" he gestures to the other bags.

"Oh, yes, absolutely," I respond brightly, but I feel totally rejected. I'm just as important as Pierre. Am I? Stop. Not true. I will not lie to myself about this. He may have been doing this longer, but I'm just as important to Sinder Ella Soles. Yes. That feels light and I'm choosing it.

I impatiently wait for the bellboy to prepare my bag claim ticket. Then I grab it from his hands and rush to catch up with Lucy and Pierre, but they have disappeared.

Feeling deflated, I walk alone down the red carpet to the main entrance. I scan quickly back and forth hoping to see Pierre. I passed CBS and find a great place to stop and watch actors' interviews. Oh, there's Reese. I lift my arm half-way to wave and then place it back down remembering in my current reality I don't know her. I pause for a moment, inhaling the oneness of this delicious moment, despite being abandoned by Pierre. Ashton would have never done that to me. Not that I'm comparing—just saying.

An E! TV reporter has suddenly appeared in front of me. "Mrs. Hunt!" I swivel my head around to find Mrs. Hunt wondering if that's Ashton's wife. And before I know it a swarm of paparazzi is rushing towards me.

19

What?

"Mrs. Hunt!" The reporter jabs the microphone at my mouth. "So, I'm here with Rachael Hunt, wife of producer and actor Ashton Hunt. Is it true that you are the master designer behind this season's phenomenal Sinder Ella Soles?"

"Excuse me?" I start shaking my head in denial. I look again for Pierre to rescue me but he can't be found. Then I begin to nod as if I have stage fright. Where's Pierre? What does the reporter mean "Mrs. Hunt?" And he knows about Sinder Ella?

"Yes, she is the master designer," Pierre runs up and comments without hesitation.

"Did Ashton inspire your decision to join Pierre Brock in this new venture?" the reporter asks.

"Actually, no, it was Pierre Brock," I reply without thinking and warmly gesture to him.

Pierre looks absolutely stunned when he hears the

name Ashton. He's standing there like a deer in headlights with his mouth half open.

"Are you glad to have Mrs. Hunt join your team this year?" the reporter asks Pierre.

He nods and nods with this dumbfounded look on his face, "Um. Yes. Of course I am," he finally responds as he puts his arm around me.

"Will Ashton be joining you two tonight?" the reporter asks as if he already knows the answer is no.

"No. Actually, he's off on location and soon coming from Fiji. Pierre is accompanying me tonight," I reply with confidence.

"Ooo laaa laaa. I can feel the emotion. Thank you. Take care. Have fun tonight," he announces as he completes the interview.

"Wait, sir, Pierre is just my business partner!" I yell, but he's already talking to his next guest.

I turn to Pierre feeling a mixture of sick, confused and angry. Finally, I ask, "What's happening here?"

"I'm not sure," he replies slowly.

"So, do you think everything I remember is true?" I ask in total frustration and start to walk off the red carpet.

Pierre is trailing after me when I angrily say, "Wasn't there something that you wanted to tell me? What was that? Was that about this?" I ask feeling anger brewing inside about this lie. I start pushing people, no matter who they are. I say under my breath, "I'm sorry, Brad and Angelina. I didn't mean to just walk between you."

I see Reese from afar, "Hi, Rachael!" she waves.

I smile and give her a quick wave as I force myself to calmly exit the red velvet ropes. Then I let out a deep sigh and feel a nudge of gratitude for the proof that I'm not completely delusional.

"Rachael, stop, wait!" Pierre yells as I start running off.

I speed walk away whispering under my breath, "What the hell is going on?"

"Wait! Stop! Rachael, can you slow down a bit?" Pierre runs after me breathlessly. "Look. I didn't know all the details. I didn't know anything about Ashton. I didn't know you really were married to him." He pauses and then convincingly says, "Honestly! I had no clue. Rachael stop. I love you."

I halt suddenly and turn to face him. We both pause in confusion. "What? What do you mean you didn't know all the details?" I yell as we nearly knock heads.

"The fact of the matter is," he swallows, "when I agreed to take you into my business I didn't know the whole story. I honestly didn't know Jake wasn't your real husband." He's shaking his head in denial. "Jake asked me not to tell you about the agreement. He told me he was doing it for you to support your dreams of being a designer. I knew something was off, but his love for you seemed sincere."

This is completely crazy. I am standing here surrounded by beauty and what felt like oneness, and I had thought it would be one of the greatest moments of my life, but now it seems to be a big joke. And all of a sudden, old feelings regarding my self-worth come rushing in. I feel like a stupid little girl, a big fake and a fraud. Who am I to think I co-owned a footwear company? Who am I? I say to myself, which used to be a statement instead of a question; however, today I respond to it as a question. I don't know and I'm not sure if I should allow anything to define me. I know that this is—well, just what it is—maybe a silly game lead by an ex-boyfriend, or maybe some divine intervention to create change. Whatever it is, I can receive it.

"Look, Jake is not the enemy. He has been there for me," I say acknowledging Jake, but not really sure why I have any need to do so.

Pierre with an adoring smile says, "Yes. And he's behind this adventurous story," he nods and we both take a breath. "I made the assumption that if I would have told you that it would have destroyed the possibility of us creating Sinder Ella Soles, and I'm sorry."

I sit back with my arms crossed, "No, that's not true. You could have told me. You know me. You could have told me and we still could have created Sinder Ella."

"It's more complicated than that, Rachael," Pierre places his thumb and two-fingers together above his nose to his third eye.

"Okay. I give. How is it more complicated? Could it really be more complicated than being blindsided by a reporter?" I ask in total frustration.

"I'm really sorry about that." He takes a long pause and frowns, "Hey, when were you planning to meet Ashton after his trip to Fiji?" He gives me a wry look redirecting the conversation.

"Umm, let's see. He said it would be easy to remember

five-five-five: May fifth at five p.m. at the Eiffel Tower" I look at my watch. Um. Would that be tonight?" I look up. "Yes. I guess it would be," I reply feeling this big revelation flowing through my body. "In about five hours?" I say in question. "Pierre, wait, I need answers. Tell me what you know. I need to know now."

"Okay. At five tonight, you will be in Ashton's arms. I guarantee it," he grins at me. "We better make some plans." He pulls out his phone and places it at his ear.

My mind is suddenly preoccupied with thoughts about Ashton. Why wasn't he looking for me? Where was he? Wouldn't he have engaged all media outlets to find me? Or was he really away from all technology? Then a thought crosses my mind and I vaguely look at Pierre on the phone and suddenly out of my mouth comes, "Ashton's the father?"

"What?" Pierre says removing the phone from his ear.

"I'm pregnant. I was trying to tell you, but the time wasn't right. I mean with the trip and divorce and everything," I say.

"Oh wow! Congratulations! I'm so happy for you and Ashton," he says genuinely and places the phone back to his ear. As I hear him ask for the nearest helicopter landing, a smile spreads across my face. He's as spontaneously crazy as Ashton. No wonder I find him irresistibly attractive. He presses the end button and looks up at me, "We need to hail a taxi."

I let out my biggest NY taxi whistle.

"Impressive," he responds.

"Tell me everything you know," I demand as we're seated in the taxi.

"I will explain. I promise. Let's make sure we are on our way to Paris first," he says giving the driver directions to the helicopter landing.

"Okay." I look out the window and let down my gauntlet of anger. I'm going to see Ashton tonight. I can't stop smiling.

I see a sprinkling of rain on the window. It reminds me of the night Ashton left for Fiji. It was Ashton's big night and I didn't even want to be there with him. I used to be so selfish and self-centered. I know that I'm different now. I won't treat people that way. I have this kindness inside that I've never had before. I hope he forgives me.

"That's it, we're here," Pierre points for the taxi driver to stop. Before Pierre steps from the cab he creates a makeshift umbrella from his coat and holds it over me as we exit. This brings up a bunch of old memories. I remember my ruined leather jacket the night I met Lucy in wardrobe. I remember the sweet light-hearted nature Ashton had the night he left. He was doing his best to keep things fun, easy and joyful for me that night despite the trip—and I was such a jerk to him.

"What do you think has happened in Ashton's life over the last five weeks?" I ask as my Sinder Ella heel slowly sinks in a puddle.

Then suddenly without warning I slip backwards. Pierre's left arm catches me as my left sandal flies off my foot. He scoops me up and we both step away from the taxi and hear a loud crunch! Shit. The taxi has just flattened my sandal.

"Noooooooo!" I screech, but it's too late.

"It's okay. You can make another, love," Pierre speaks

warmly as he lifts me in his arms and carries me through the rain towards the helicopter. When we get close, the rain becomes worse from the helicopter propeller.

Once we're seated and strapped in I start laughing hysterically. I'm a mess. My blue chiffon dress is ruined and it's completely see-through when wet. This typically would frustrate the hell out of me, but today I find it insanely funny.

"What's so funny?" Pierre asks.

"Well, I just realized all our clothes are in Cannes and look at me," I gesture to my dress.

"Oh, is this funny?" he asks. "You look beautiful—a little like a scarecrow." He pulls out his handkerchief and offers some help with my running mascara.

I take out my mirrored compact from my bag and look. I respond with a burst of deep intense laughter.

Pierre dabs some spring water on his handkerchief and says, "Look up." He begins to gently wipe below my lower lashes. "You know, Ashton is one lucky guy. I bet he's going out of his mind not being with you." He pauses, "Now, look down." He continues delicately clearing the smeared mascara from my face. "If Ashton's not missing you he needs his head examined." Pierre sits back and looks at my face, "Ah, much better. Now you look absolutely gorgeous, my dear," he says laying on his French accent.

"Thank you," I smile.

"Hey. Maybe we can find you something to wear when we arrive. I heard there's a store there called Blissful Being." He nods and with a grin says, "It's my new high-end clothing line designed to show off your footwear."

"Oh, wow. I didn't know you had a clothing line. Tell me more," I ask curiously.

"Yes. It's my first line! That's why I flew out early. I'm sorry I didn't tell you. I didn't know how you would react," Pierre says in an apologetic tone.

"It's fine. I'm so happy for you," I trail off redirecting his focus back to what happened after my fall. "So, tell me—you said you only knew part of the story. What do you know?"

"Are you sure you want to hear this?" He takes a breath.

"I need to know. Yes. I want to know," I reply with a hint of anger, but it's not directed at him—it's about this whole crazy mess.

"A few weeks before your fall, Jake scheduled an appointment with me about a big business possibility and joint venture. As a person who is always open to greater possibilities, I was thrilled with the idea of meeting him." He looks to the sky. "As you may know, sometimes what comes out someone's mouth is very different than what what's really going on. I perceived this, but I couldn't sense what was really going on—and I loved the idea."

"And—?" I probe.

"So, when we met he told me about his wife, Rachael. He said she studied design at UCLA and loved my work. He said that she had deeply desired to meet and work with me for years."

I stop him. "Wait. He told you I was his *wife*?" I emphasize wife so loud Pierre nearly jumps.

"Like I said, I knew something was off, but didn't know

what. I thought it would be fun to bring in a new designer, especially from the designs he showed me," he continues.

"Stop. So, Jake had my designs. How did he know I wanted to work with you?" I ask curiously.

"Well, I'm not sure if it's only Jake behind this little scheme. I think there are others involved," he replies.

"Why?"

"I'm getting to that," he replies quickly.

"Fine," I reply impatiently.

"I was very excited to bring in a new designer, but then I learned that his wife—you—recently had a fall that left you with amnesia. Still not a big deal. Until he told me that he wanted me to act as if you had been a partner in the company for a while. Weird, right?"

"Yes. Okaaay," I say as I let out a frustrated exhale.

"Then to reduce my risk he said he wanted this so bad for you that he would completely pay for your shoe line including manufacturing equipment, and the line must be called 'Sinder Ella.'"

I gasp, "I never told Jake that." I look up trying to remember when I thought of the name. "Hmmm. Actually, I think it was with Ashton when the name first came up. It was during one of our first dates. I don't remember saying anything to Jake about it." I frown. "Yes, it was Ashton that came up with that name," I say clarifying. "How did Jake know?"

"Weird. He even had designs for us to start creating so you would think you were the founder," Pierre responds while in deep thought.

"Ohmigod." I gulp. "I drew a lot in college." Then I think about the design I first saw in the bag at the hospital, "But that just doesn't make sense. I drew the 'Jasmine' design in my journal a little over a year ago. I was in Hawaii with Ashton to be exact." I trail off. "Do you think Ashton is involved?"

"Hmmm. That's interesting question. What do you think?" Pierre asks.

"No. What other questions can I ask to get to the bottom of this?" I ask Pierre.

"Well, let me continue with what I know and we'll see what comes up," he responds.

"Great," I nod for him to continue.

"Jake also said he dearly loved you and wanted to make all your dreams come true. It was incredibly romantic and convincing," Pierre says.

"Of course it would be, he's a lawyer." In deep thought I look down. Pierre starts caressing my back which causes me to rudely jerk away. "I'm sorry Pierre. I know this isn't your fault. I'm just mad."

"No. It is my fault. I agreed to conspire when I knew something didn't feel right," he says with sincerity.

"We're here!" Yells the pilot as we touch down on the landing pad.

"Fantastic!" I say dreaming of Ashton.

"What time is it?" Pierre asks.

"Two fifteen Paris time," replies the pilot.

"Is that enough time to get us from here to the Eiffel Tower?" I ask anxiously.

"Yes, but it'll be close. Grab a limo or cab from the landing gate," he points in the direction for us to find ground transportation.

"Thanks," Pierre hands the pilot five hundred Euros and in the same breath yells to me, "Go, go, go!"

I step out of the helicopter and notice the rain has subsided. There are deep puddles of water and mud everywhere. Suddenly Pierre swoops my barefoot body into his arms and starts running like mad, "Don't get any ideas?"

"Ha. Ha. I'll try not to," I reply back with a smile looking directly into his eyes.

When we reach the gate Pierre sets me under the awning while he arranges transportation to the tower. I had envisioned this evening very differently several weeks ago, but for some reason it feels amazingly phenomenal the way it is right now. No rain, wind or other elements can take me down—and honestly inside I feel happy, joyful and fulfilled knowing I'm going to see Ashton very soon.

"Hey, good looking, would you like a ride?" Pierre asks with a grin standing in front of a black limo and driver.

"That was fast," I reply with a big smile.

He opens the door and says, "Yes, money and fashion buy quick response, eh?"

"Yes. Thank you. Thank you so much," I respond genuinely.

20

Love

My heart gives an almighty flip when we reach the Eiffel Tower and the reality of reuniting with Ashton is so close. It feels like a dream floating on a cloud. I can't believe I'm here, especially after the past five weeks of chaos.

"Get in the line. I'll get you a ticket." Pierre demands, snapping me from my daydream.

"Okay," I say staring at the elevator line to the top. I consider taking the stairs until I examine my bare feet and decide waiting will be a great idea. There was no time to get new shoes or new clothes in our rush from the airport.

A few moments later Pierre is back with two tickets and joins me in line. I look at him uncomfortably.

"Of course I won't go all the way up with you, but I wanted to be here with you, until you want me to go."

"How did you know I was thinking that?" I give him a quirky smile.

"Ah. That psychic thing I have," he replies with a smile.

"Oh. Yes. Well, you know, I put the thought in your head," I laugh.

"Of course you did," he replies.

We reach the front of the line, and as I prepare to get on the elevator Pierre takes off his Brock Soles and hands them to me. "You will want shoes. I will see you some time soon." Pierre responds knowing that it is time for us to part.

"Thank you," I nod and give him a hug.

When I arrive at the top of the tower my heart is racing so hard I think I'm going to burst. I step off the elevator and look all around; I don't see Ashton. I look down and feel a little silly in Pierre's shoes. Suddenly my eyes are covered by two hands. I gasp and turn. There he is. It's him. He looks so good. He's sporting a white button down linen shirt with designer jeans. He's tanned and lean. His hair has grown to a mid-length and it's sun-bleached from the Fiji sun. He's even wearing a casual hand-crafted bracelet. My eyes drop to his footwear. He's wearing the same style Brock Soles that I am. It's all unbelievable. It's my Ashton in front of me. I stare at him dazzlingly as he envelops me in a full body hug.

"Hi baby," I hear in my ear as he kisses my earlobe. "God, I've missed you so much. Let's not do this again ever."

"No. Let's not. Ashton, I missed you too. So much," I whisper in his ear on the verge of tears.

"I never want to leave you for that long, baby," Ashton says endearingly.

"Yay." I sing light-heartedly.

"So, what happened? And why are you water-logged

and wearing men's shoes?" he smiles gesturing to our matching footwear.

"Ha. Oh. On the rush over here the cab crushed one of my sandals and Pierre gave me his," I say lightheartedly. "Can you believe that?"

"Pierre?" Ashton asks jokingly.

"Ha. You have no idea what I've been through these past few weeks." I laugh and hug him tighter. "Just hold me."

"Alright," Ashton replies with a smile, "but then I can't give you these," he says sadly holding a wrapped gift the size of a shoe box.

"Wow!" I giggle in surprise ripping the wrapping from the box. I stare at the label top, "Sinder Ella Soles?" Well, now I know he's not a part of this elaborate skit—unless this is his way of telling me. I stand there waiting for him to say something.

"I know how you like Brock Soles. A friend found me these for you. I couldn't resist. Remember when you wanted to name your line Cinderella?" He says with exuberant joy.

"Yeah. Um. Yeah." I stare at the box and I don't have words. I watch as Ashton slowly removes the little bow and lifts the lid. I see my Jasmine design. It's my first design in purple with three straps and a buckle. I pull out one sandal and observe all the unique characteristics. Then I spot it. There's an unusual charm on the buckle. I look a little closer. No, there's not. There's a platinum diamond five carat ring staring at me. "What? Why?" I say taking the ring from the buckle.

"Why?" Ashton takes the ring from me and drops to

one knee. "Rachael Marie Hunt will you marry me?" he asks right there.

I place my hand to my head. What's going on? And after a moment I finally say, "What? Aren't we already married? Ashton? Weren't we married in Vegas five years ago? I'm totally confused."

"Apparently not. It turns out that the chapel where we were married did not have an ordained minister. We weren't married that night in Vegas. They sent a certified letter to the office and my assistant Jane called me yesterday. I thought I would surprise you. Will you officially marry me?" Ashton asks.

"No. No. No." I shake my head and mumble in disoriented confusion and disbelief.

"No?" Ashton replies as if I responded to the proposal.

Tourists are staring at us. I hear their whispers all around us. I hear one say, "It's that movie star, Ashton Hunt." And another says, "Is that his wife?"

"Yes. Of course. Yes. I'll marry you!" I finally say as Ashton begins to place the ring on my finger. I take a deep breath feeling relieved to be with Ashton and knowing that he remembers the Vegas chapel and I'm not delusional.

"I always wanted a diamond like this from you," I say staring at the big fat rock.

"I know." Ashton twirls and swings me as if we just finished a dance. I love when he does this.

"It's beautiful. It's so beautiful Ashton," I say admiring the ring.

Ashton bends down, removes Pierre's shoes from my

feet and replaces them with the sandals. "You'll have to give me the 4-1-1 about this Pierre later," he says as we hear a loud burst. "Look!" He points to the sky.

"Déjà vu," I say watching the amazing display of lights.

"Yes!" he replies.

"Thank you," I whisper with a little shiver.

"I love you," he replies "Are you cold?"

"Yes. Let's get out of here. I'd love some awesome Parisian food," I nod with pure joy and excitement.

He lifts me up and carries me over the threshold of the elevator.

"Woo Hoo!" I let out with a feeling of radiant bliss.

"Congratulations," says a man on the elevator.

"Thank you sir," Ashton replies to him.

I can't stop smiling. For some strange reason I get this sense that Ashton has changed. My workaholic-actor has vanished—the hyperactive, adrenaline-rich Ashton has disappeared and now I have my Ashton back. The real Ashton.

21

The Difference Between Bliss and Judged Bliss

IT TURNS OUT TO BE the most magical night of my life. I put on my brand-new dress that Ashton and I found in a little shop just minutes from the tower. I find Ashton dressed in a new fine white suit. We go to a magical French restaurant—which was exactly as I imagined by the way.

During dinner, I allow Ashton to keep things light by sharing his fun adventures from Fiji. He went surfing, horseback riding, scuba diving and snorkeling. He shares his Fiji stories in the usual Ashton way, so it creates this beautiful picture for me. He's always shared his stories this way, but this is the first time in years I am capable of receiving them—I feel as if I'm experiencing them with him.

As I listen and engage in the vision I'm also very aware of my present state. I feel like the princess who escaped the evil Jake-guarded castle. I feel so lucky. And I'm also so grateful for the journey with Pierre. I'm a very different person now—and the weird thing is I feel Ashton is different too. He's the man I deeply and truly love. I relish in this thought, when I hear him say, "I really missed you, baby. I wish you had come with me. I understand why you chose not to, but still. So what happened while I was gone? I tried to get in touch a couple of days ago. Where were you? You didn't return my calls? I called Silvia and she said you were out after I called your mobile probably twenty times. You never answered," he says and checks his phone. "Actually I called thirty-one times."

"She did?" I say in shock. And then say under my breath to myself, "Silvia didn't know I had disappeared for five weeks?" Did I just say that out loud?

Ashton straightens up in shock, "What?"

"What?" I respond innocently, not sure if I want to go down the rabbit hole right now.

"What did you just say? Disappeared?" Ashton says, "Is this why Katie sent me a letter?"

"She did?" I shake my head in denial. "Ohmigod, Ashton, it's a crazy long story. Tell me what the letter said," I ask, surprising myself that I waited this long to share the drama.

"Well, the gist of it was that I needed to get back. She said there was an accident and you were physically fine, but you were acting a little strange. That was five days ago. And when you didn't return my calls I started to become a little worried. I didn't know if you were going to show up at the tower. I thought maybe something changed between us."

I nod.

"Did something change between us? What happened? What was that about disappearing?" he asks with intense concern.

"You don't know anything that happened? Truth? You don't know about Sinder Ella Soles? You bought me a pair? I thought, um, maybe you knew something," I probe.

He gives me a look that shows that he has no idea what I'm talking about. "I have no clue what you are talking about. Sam's assistant sent me those to give you. She thought you'd like them."

"Oh. You don't know. You aren't in on this? Are you?" I declare and ask the question at the same time.

"Know what? I know you had an accident from Katie's letter, is there more?" Ashton responds.

"Oh. Ashton, there is so much you don't know," I respond shaking my head in denial.

"Are you okay?" Ashton asks with a deep concern.

"Okay? Um, yes, from the accidents I'm fine," I say as if the whole thing is not a big deal.

"So, what else is going on? What don't I know?" he asks with intensity.

"I don't know where to start. And now I sort of don't want to get into it. I just want to be with you—in the yummy essences of you. Can we talk about this later?" I say smiling and wincing at the same time. I don't want to lose this spacious feeling of joy and bliss when I go into the story. Pierre says that I should never go into the story—maybe this is one of those times?

"Oh love. Please tell me. I want to know what happened. It really scared me when I got the letter and then I couldn't find you. And now you don't want to talk about it. Rachael, for God's sake what's going on?" his face has become pale.

"Um. Okay. Just listen and ask questions when I finish. Okay?" I ask so I can get through this quickly.

Ashton nods.

I tell him the story from the accident at the studio when he leaves, to the shocking hospital awakening where Jake and his daughter Christina acted as my family—which brings to me the sudden obvious realization that I am not actually Christina's mom. That explains the emotional distance between us, but adds to my confusion—how can Jake have a five year old? I tell Ashton about Katie's party and the paparazzi-induced car accident afterwards—as that was my first indication that I may not have memory loss. I leave out the part about being an owner of Sinder Ella Soles and my relationship with Pierre—I'll tell him that later. I mean, geesh, he already knew I had a crush on the famous designer, I don't need to feed any fires. I also decide to leave out the pregnancy.

"Oh shit," he says several times during the story and again right now. "Who do you think arranged this? Jake? Jake and Katie? He has plenty of money to buy off a lot of people. He was pissed when you left him. And even worse when he knew you were with me. But how does this benefit him? Did he really think the truth would never come out?

What a jerk. Arg! I can't believe this." Ashton says as his thoughts just fall out of his mouth.

"Actually, Jake and I have become friends. He is obviously a part of this. Oh, and get this. His firm partner is Katie. How funny is that? I would guess both of them were in on it," I say as if trying to tell him that's how she was involved and why she wrote the note.

"But how did Katie get my address in Fiji? Who gave it to her?" Ashton asks looking for answers.

"Oh. The journal! I bet Katie has my dragon journal. Of course," I gasp in realization.

"Dragon journal?" Ashton asks.

"I found this awesome blank journal at Jake's. I was so confused about what was happening to me, I started to keep track of things in this journal. Your address was in there. I wrote it in there a few days after I found it. I was questioning why I knew this exact address. I start to write a letter, which was also in the journal, but I never sent it," I say with a new awareness. "I was afraid if someone found it I would be put in a looney bin."

He nods, "So, Katie must have been a part of this little scheme. Ha, if she wasn't she would have asked you why you were living with Jake and not me. So, we know Jake and Katie were a part of this, who else?" I can feel anger brewing inside him as he states the facts.

"Actually I thought it might be someone you knew. There were things they knew from my present life with you. And there were paparazzi. Ashton, I thought you might have been involved." I grasp with a realization, "What if it was a collaborative paparazzi group that got Jake involved? They've been watching my every move. No. You don't think? Do you?" I ask Ashton.

"Shit. I think I know who else may be involved. We'll find out," he states with potency I hardly ever see in him. I can tell his head is spinning with possibilities about what we can do next.

"Who?" I ask.

"Let's not worry about it tonight. I'm going to get to the bottom of this. I promise you." He lifts his glass, "Tonight is for us. Here's to us. We are oneness. Oneness, once again. I love you, baby." And with that our glasses clink and he leans across the table to give me kiss.

We stay out for hours. We drink, dance to the live band, feed each other chocolate truffles, and talk about everything except my altered life and who's involved.

When we return to the hotel we're both laughing and tripping over each other's feet. Our lips are randomly touching and my eyes are half open and half shut.

"Mrs. Hunt?" A French man at the front desk is yelling at me as we enter. "There's an urgent message from a Mr. Brock. He's called several times and continues to state immediate urgency."

My knees become weak and my heart flutters hard when I hear his name. "Um—" I start to speak and then let Ashton finish.

"Mus-not-be-fir-us-sir-we-don't-know-a-brock-in-Paris," Ashton laughs. He's so cute when he slurs his words.

I play along rolling my eyes feeling a little guilty for not telling Ashton about Pierre.

"Here's the number," says the concierge shoving the pink message slip in my face.

"No thanks," I say waving him off. I giggle back to Ashton and we wait for the lift.

When we arrive at the room it's clear we are both pretty drunk. Maybe a six on the drunk scale of one to ten. Ashton is stumbling all over me and himself to find the door card—and I drop to my knees laughing hysterically.

"This has been one of the best nights of my life," I say as he opens the room door.

"Oh, love, it's not over yet," he laughs as he unzips the back of my dress and slams the door shut with the back of his foot. My beautiful dress falls to the ground as he's gently kissing the nape of my neck. I allow him to caress, fondle, and envelope my body with yummy Ashton love. His eyes get this meaningful look and he whispers, "I'm glad you're here. I mean you are really here."

"Yes," I giggle.

"No, I mean it. I was starting to feel that our lifestyle was killing the playful you. The one I fell in love with. Now, you are really here. You. The Rachael I met five years ago was fun and playful, but she was still pretending to be better than she thought she was. Today, you are really you and really here," he states looking directly in my eyes.

"It feels good to be here now with you. I love you, Ashton," I say sweetly.

"I love you too. And now is the time to be with the love of my life. Right here, right now. I give myself completely to you," he declares grandly.

"Yay!" I squeak when we tumble to the floor. Our bodies are intertwined. I catch a glimpse in the mirror and think to myself. This is what's real. This is my life. This is me. This is us. Yes. Yes. Yes.

22

Choices, Choices, Choices

AFTER THE BEST LOVE-MAKING of my life I lay with my cheek on Ashton's chest. "Yummy," I whisper.

"Rachael, what happened? You are different—like really different. You are more real. More beautiful. More you! I feel you are really behind your eyes and not trying to resist, defend and fight against everything. I've missed you. I feel like I haven't seen you like I am now. It's awesome. What changed?" Ashton smiles with a joy in his eyes.

"Um," I think about all the conscious perspectives and viewpoints taught to me by Pierre and for a moment I consider telling Ashton, but instead I say, "I guess I realized I was trying to be what I thought others wanted me to be instead of being me." I trail off.

"I see," Ashton says as we hear a tap, tap, tap on the door.

"No housekeeping needed," Ashton yells to the door and then looks to me, "Didn't I put the do not disturb sign in the door slot?"

I nod as we hear louder rap on the door.

"It's Pierre," the voice yells outside the door.

Suddenly, I snap out of my afterglow and bolt upright. I look at Ashton in dismay.

"What? Who is this Pierre guy anyway?" Ashton asks curiously checking the clock. "What the hell?"

"Rachael, it's me. Open the door. It's an emergency," yells Pierre from outside the door. I flop back on the bed in frustration. Just let me be in my amazing dream. Go away please, I quietly plea inside my mind.

"Who is that, Rachael?" Ashton whispers again to me now as a real question.

I open my mouth and then close it as a way to stall for words.

"I know you're in there," Pierre yells from the hall.

Shit. "Fine. Just a minute," I yell to the door.

"Who is he?" Ashton repeats loudly now for the third time.

"It's Pierre Brock. You know—the shoe designer," I say in frustration putting on Ashton's shirt and boxer shorts.

"Pierre *Brock*? Why is he here in the middle of the night? What is it that I don't know?"

"Long story." I roll my eyes at him. "Really long. We became friends." Then with one hand on the door knob and the other one on Ashton's heart I say, "Ashton, there's something I need to tell you and I will after you meet Pierre. Please stay open-minded. Nothing happened like you might be thinking." I open the door for Pierre to enter.

"Of course. When have I not been open-minded?" Ashton says under his breath as Pierre comes in.

"Cute," Pierre says eyeing me up and down in Ashton's attire.

"This better be good," I say feeling incredibly awkward having both Pierre and Ashton in the same room. Just yesterday I thought Pierre might be my guy and now my life is completely different.

"Sit down," Pierre demands in haste.

"Well, yes sir." I salute him facetiously as I wander over to the bed and plop down as if I'm obeying his command.

"Listen. A story has been leaked to the press. It's going to be all over the news tomorrow." Pierre looks back and forth between Ashton and me. He holds out his right hand and says to Ashton, "It's nice to finally meet you. I've heard a lot about you."

"It's a pleasure to meet you, Mr. Brock. We're both huge fans of your work. Rachael has been for years." Ashton looks endearingly over at me and comments on my behalf.

"Pierre. What exactly are you saying?" I work to refocus both of them.

Ashton nods for Pierre to begin.

"Um. Well, the story about us has been leaked to the tabloids in the States." He takes a deep breath.

"What story exactly?" I interrupt nervously not knowing if I want to know.

"The scandal. How you were tricked into believing you were with Jake. How you were made to believe this new reality," he trails off and looks down, "And there's more." I've never seen him look so worried. He looks directly at me. "Look Rachael, I don't want to hurt you. I want our friendship to continue after all this. You know me. I wouldn't do anything to hurt you. You've become my best friend." He looks at Ashton, "Both of you."

"Pierre, stop! What are you staying?" I ask with a nervous flip. I look to Ashton and can tell he's thinking the worst.

"There are pictures. Pictures when you were sick and I drove you home. Pictures of us dancing at the charity ball. Pictures after the ball," he looks me directly in the eyes and continues, "And pictures with us really close in the limo. Shall I go on? They don't portray our relationship correctly, if you know what I mean?" Pierre replies.

"Shit," I whisper under my breath during a long unbearable silence. My hands begin to tremble. My head feels hot then cold. I look at Ashton and I can tell his mind is racing with questions.

Finally, Ashton breaks tension, "What are you saying they show your relationship 'incorrectly'? What is your relationship?" he calmly asks.

Pierre looks at me for permission to respond.

I look down and shake my head in disbelief. "Augh. This can't be happening on top of everything that has already happened," I mumble.

"Like romantic pictures?" Ashton asks. I can tell he's thinking we had an affair. And although Ashton would probably be fine with it, he would not be fine with the world knowing it.

"Well, here's the thing," I turn to Ashton. "Remember I told you about the hospital and Jake and how it was portrayed that I was in this loveless marriage with him. Well, Pierre and I met and we became very close. He was there for me." I stop to take a breath hoping someone will jump in before I make matters worse. I'm ready to hear Ashton say it's not a big deal and it's going to be okay, or that we've been in the tabloids thousands of times and we're going to be fine. But he doesn't, so I continue. I look to Pierre as I spill my guts, "We didn't have an affair, but we were intimate and close at times. That's just who Pierre is." And then I make matters worse and say how I feel about Pierre, "We are very close. We are this sort-of oneness." And then I try to save myself as I look at Ashton and say, "You know. Like you and me. You know how it is. Right?" I ramble then finally shut my mouth.

"Oh wow," Ashton drops his shaking head in his hands.

I put a hand on Ashton's back and warmly start the reassurance line, "Look baby, it is what it is. We've been in the tabloids thousands of times. We're going to be fine." I calmly and confidently say, "We're going to be better than fine. We're going to exceed all perceptions. What is so right about this?"

"Rachael, yes, I know. I was just thinking of how we were going to change this by manipulating the hell out of the paparazzi. I'm not willing to take this anymore," Ashton powerfully states.

"Awesome. I'm in. What ideas do you have?" Pierre pipes in.

"Really? What happened? You don't usually fight. You usually allow them to say it with no viewpoint."

"Well," Ashton takes a long deep breath. "Let's just say

it's time to create a new image. It's time for me to change the lies. If there are lies out there about us we might as well create them."

"Really? Because it seems everyone really loves the Ashton you are portrayed to be," I say.

"Well, that's the thing. Sam was boxing me into his beautiful portrayal. I'm tired of pretending I don't care when I really do," he finally says with a deep sigh. "I fired him a few weeks before I left for Fiji. I told him I'd do the new film, but after that I was done working with him. He was pretty pissed."

"Sam Howard?" I ask.

"He went crazy. I bet he's behind this and is trying to use this scandal to ruin me. He could have easily recruited photographers and paparazzi to follow us. I'm afraid there may be lots of stories coming out. So, we need to do whatever it takes to mess with them."

"I knew there was something up with him," I nod. "What do you mean mess with them?"

"Well, Sam and I have built my career on transformational experiences, consciousness stories and inspiration, so when stories of insanity, affairs, scandal, fights, even pictures come out we need to tell them the story we want published," he looks down in thought. "And if it looks like you are having an affair with Pierre we can have even more fun with them," he says with a smile.

"Don't you say, consciousness is everything without fixed positions and judgment? So, when they judge you as a certain persona isn't that an opportunity to show them there's another way? What if this could be more expansive for consciousness than we ever thought possible?" I smile and actually believe it.

"I like this new side of you," he smiles. "And that is a possibility for some—what else can be changed because we are choosing this manipulative story? As I see it there is no conclusive stop to this—when we come to conclusion it stops the change and it becomes a limitation. Let's keep playing with people for the greater planetary consciousness," Ashton replies.

"Aren't you afraid of what people will think?" I ask Ashton realizing that what I just said is all about judgment.

"No. I don't care what people think. That's their choice to think and their choice to come to those lies and conclusions about me. There's no freedom in that. And we can choose to tell stories and control the possible expected conclusions," he replies with clarity, but I'm not sure I got it.

"Ashton, look at me," I request.

"Yes," he turns to face me.

"Do you remember our first date?" I grab his hand.

"Yes, of course!" He responds slowly, not sure where I'm going with this.

"You asked me if I was a dreamer. You asked me why I was hiding such a beautiful secret. You asked me if I was willing to deny what was true about me. It's been a skipping record in my head for years. You put it in my head the first day we met and I continued to deny it for the years we were together. When my life was turned upside down the last few weeks, I found myself remembering that experience. And

209

suddenly I stopped denying and justifying why I wasn't choosing my dreams." I pause hoping he will stop me before I become emotional. "Well, I'm starting to create my life in that way. I'm starting to receive the whispers and ideas that are possible—and I'm starting to choose those whispers as true possibility. Things are unfolding like magic. You always said it would be magical, and I denied that. I'm sorry I wasn't listening. Anyway, I share that so you know I'm ready to see the situation as what it is and mess with them dynamically. So, what will we do?"

"Sweetie, those inner whispers are your GPS! The universe gives you what you choose when you ask. The only problem is some people don't ask and choose from those whispers and instead they choose their fears," he laughs.

I start laughing as well. And now the three of us are hysterically laughing about all of this. "Yes, so I'm a little slow. Now, I'm living in a state of constant creation, not a state of completion. How fun is that? In some ways, I'm actually instantly actualizing something into the physical." I give him a quirky smile. "And, Pierre, I'm so really grateful for you. The past few weeks you've really been there for me. You've shown me this way of being in the world that I never thought was possible. And how I can be present with all the uncomfortable gunk of life and create more change than I ever thought I was capable of," I give Pierre a sincere, caring hug.

"So tell me, what have you magically actualized?" He asks curiously.

"Okay. I hope you are ready, Ashton." I reply with a

wink as I review my recent altered-life revelations. I take a breath and drop all my defensive walls and say, "Number one, I'm a famous footwear designer. My footwear line just had its debut in Cannes." I make the statement and wait for his reaction, but there isn't one. He nods with a validating acknowledgement. I watch him drop into a relaxed state of receiving more like this from me. "Number two, I instantly became a mother, you know, a mother to Christina— although now I guess that doesn't really count," I trail off still avoiding mentioning the pregnancy. "And!" I grandly announce, "Number three I've instantly become a part of an elite business team with a lot of respect, impact, purpose, and inspiration. These are all things I've been asking for and now I have them. Oh, yes, and number four, I have reunited with the love of my life—you. You see what I mean? And that's just the physical external stuff; my internal changes are endless." I reply not even needing his validation.

"Famous footwear designer," Ashton repeats with a smile. "You just had to choose it. Rach, you're phenomenal, you'd just forgotten who you were born to be."

"Hey and since this isn't a crazy, delusional dream of mine. I can continue to choose it," I respond in deep thought.

"Absolutely! Especially now that you're involved with Pierre Brock," he says casually.

"Yes, I am," I say giving Ashton a big smile, wondering if there is some inkling of jealousy there?

"And by the way I totally adore how you two are today. I can tell there's a deep caring you have for each other. And

I'm personally happy to see that we can be together in this way," Ashton smiles.

"I love you so much, Ashton," I say giving him a giant hug of love and gratitude.

23

New Way

"Stop." Pierre announces loudly with a potency that breaks up this beautiful moment of our embrace. "Look. We have a choice," he announces. "The paparazzi are outside waiting for us. It's time to choose how we will reply. How do you want to respond?"

With my heart thumping, I look to Ashton for a response. I watch as a quirky little smile breaks from Ashton's mouth. "What? What are you thinking?" I ask.

"What story could we give them?" Ashton grins.

"Yes. What story?" I reply.

"Yes. Well they expect us to fight or hide which causes separation. So what if we gave them something juicy to write in partnership with them? This way they can sell the story and we get media exposure," Ashton replies.

"Okay." I agree and look to Pierre to see if he's in too.

"I like it," Pierre smiles.

"Okay, well this will look like a threesome when we leave this room," Ashton says."

"What would your commentary be about that?" I ask Ashton.

"What's their judgment of a threesome? What's wrong with that personal choice? You see where I'm going with this?" Ashton replies.

"Totally." I say.

"Why not? I can flirt with Pierre. He's a good looking guy," he winks at Pierre.

"I'm good with that. Will it limit my company's growth? Probably not, most designers are gay—at least I'd be willing to play both sides," Pierre winks back.

And that's what we do. We walk out together. Ashton puts his arm around Pierre and they both kiss me. We hold the pose as many cameras flash around us. Each of us openly comments on our integrated relationship story until the interest has subsided.

We arrive at Pierre's little Italian car with a new exhilaration. I have never had such a successful paparazzi encounter. Once we are seated and the car doors are closed, we break into laughter.

"That was crazy! They loved it!" Ashton laughs.

"Pierre, what did you say to the guy that asked about my relationship with Jake?" I ask.

He squints, "I said we include him in oneness as well, but he was not in bed tonight."

"Eek. That makes me a total slut," I laugh even harder.

"Oh my, we are going to blow up the media." Ashton grins and asks Pierre, "Do you think it will sell more shoes?"

"Absolutely. Do you think it will sell more movie tickets?" he responds gleefully.

"Absolutely!" Ashton laughs.

"Want to go to my place in the French hills?" Pierre asks.

"Yes," Ashton replies for us both.

✶ ✶ ✶

"We're here," Pierre announces as we arrive on his beautiful French vineyard sometime in the middle of the night. Pierre gives us a brief tour of his house and guest rooms and he bids us good night.

Once we are settled in bed Ashton turns to me and says, "I'm assuming there's more to the story that I don't know."

I nod.

"You can tell me when you are ready. I love you," he says, giving me a passionate good night kiss.

"I love you too, baby," I say as I drift off to sleep.

The next morning I wake to Ashton handing me a cup of tea and the French tabloid magazine *Closer*. I don't go through my orientation process. Today, I am awake—really awake. I'm at Pierre's vineyard home with my fiancé Ashton. He's so cute and vulnerable.

"Thanks," I reply.

"Page twelve," Ashton whispers.

I curiously leaf through the pages. I spot the spread. As I read the headline, *Ashton Hunt est un Homosexuel*, a lump forms in my throat. I scan the article. I see the picture with the three of us snuggling on the first page. The first sub-headline reads, *L'Affaire Scandaleuse*. It's a huge article spanning three full pages. As I read it, my heart leaps with

215

an unusual feeling of excitement. The story implies that Ashton has had many homosexual affairs. There are small pictures suggesting relationships with Sam and his other guy friends. I continue to read. It doesn't mention Pierre until the end of page two. And it finally mentions how Ashton has included his wife in his latest homosexual affair. "Really?" I say sarcastically to the paper throwing it down on the bed next to Ashton. I look at Ashton and I can tell he really has no opinion about it.

"It's okay. No judgment. We set it up. It's not that far off. I knew they would take a skewed angle. They always do," he says calmly.

"Yes. I guess. I'm just not sure I know us anymore," I whisper under my breath.

"Well, what's the value of defining us?" Ashton asks. "Do you really buy the lie that you don't know us because this silly article was written this way? Do you really think I'm gay?" He laughs and looks a little taken back. "I mean not that there's anything wrong with being gay, but I'm not. You are the one I choose to be with, Rachael," Ashton states grandly.

"No. That's not it. You. I mean," I ramble. "I mean we've been hiding from the paparazzi for all these years. Why the change?" I laugh and throw him on the bed.

"I'm done fighting. I'm done judging. I will show them a fabricated story to expand my message and be in the media," Ashton simply replies. "In fact I'm sick of trying to make them choose the truth, so I'm presenting them with a story, which is exactly what they are looking for," he grins.

"Got it! I'm not sure yet if I agree with it, but I get your choices around this," I nod.

My phone pings with a text message: **how is it going?** It's from Jake. I stare blankly wondering what I should say. I'm guessing he's aware that I'm with Ashton, but the message doesn't read that way.

24

Being

PIERRE IS SEATED AT his kitchen table, which is filled with fruit and pastries, when Ashton and I emerge from the bedroom.

"Help yourself," Pierre says gesturing to the spread. "Would you like some coffee?"

"Yes, thank you," Ashton replies watching Pierre pour two cups of coffee for us.

"Pierre, would you be willing to tell me how you met Rachael?" Ashton asks, making me a little anxious.

"Didn't Rachael tell you?" Pierre asks.

"No," Ashton says looking at me.

"We didn't have a lot of time last night. It's fine. You can tell him." I say to Pierre.

"Well, I've already shared with Rachael that I don't know the whole story. Meaning, I don't know why Jake set this up. I don't know if he is the only one who has masterminded this little adventure. I came in, under contract with Jake, to help Rachael grow her dream as a footwear designer. I was told Rachael had amnesia. I was asked to bring her into the company to see if it would change her and how she felt about life. I'm only sharing because I know you have questions. I have questions too and that's about all I know," Pierre says to Ashton handing him a cup of coffee.

"Holy shit," Ashton says, "This sounds a bit too coincidental. But first of all, why did you trust Jake? Why did you believe him? Why did you want to help a complete stranger this way? Did he pay you off?"

"Honestly, I was excited about her dream. I simply wanted to help Rachael with her dream. I know what it's like to have a dream inside you. And the truth is, the warming charm of Jake's offer deluded my awareness." Pierre takes a sip of coffee and continues, "I had my hesitations but my heart wanted to help Rachael."

"And I am very grateful," I nod.

"Pierre, I'm really grateful that you and Rachael have met, I just wish it wasn't through this evil manipulation," he looks at me.

"I didn't know Jake wasn't her husband. I was told Rachael was depressed partly because she never took action on her dreams as a footwear designer. He also told me he had nudged her many times before and now that her memory was wiped clean, he thought we could get her inspired to something greater." Pierre takes a breath, "It was presented in a way that seemed like I could really help her—nothing else. When I saw her first drawings I knew her original thoughts would be a contribution to Brock's Soles." He looks at up, "It seemed harmless. It seemed as if it was asked through pure love from her adoring husband. Who would really think it was this crazy fabricated scandal?"

"I see. So, she wakes up in the hospital, is told she has amnesia, and is told she was a co-owner in your company?"

"Well, not of Brock's Soles, of Sinder Ella Soles—you know, like the sandals you gave me last night?" I clarify.

"Of course! I guess there really are no coincidences. With that name, Rachael was more likely to actually believe she'd been a part of the company to begin with since that was the name we'd talked about. But if she shared all of her confusion about her memory, why didn't you tell her the truth that Jake had you create the company for her?" Ashton curiously asks.

"Unfortunately, I couldn't," Pierre says taking a large bite of his pastry. "Um. How do I say this? He offered us a million dollar contract to create it. He thought it would allow her to create her dream as a footwear designer. I was to get her going, then I would receive equity in the company. From my perspective, I was given a million dollars to bring in a gal that I would want to hire and create with anyway." He puts the pastry down and stares at Ashton seriously, "Look. I thought it was innocent. I had no idea I was doing harm to you or Rachael. I thought I was helping a loving husband. And I had no idea she would be so incredible! I had no idea what I would learn! I am so grateful for the experience, but wouldn't choose it again," Pierre warmly replies to Ashton.

"Awww—I'm so grateful for you, too." I squeal.

"Please know it wasn't about the money. Yes, I needed it

to create Sinder Ella, but that wasn't the motivation here. It was about Rachael's dream. And then it was just about her. She's a creative genius as you may already know," Pierre says genuinely to Ashton.

"Now. Before we talk with Jake is there anything else we need to talk about?" I sigh. "Ashton, what do you know? You mentioned something about Sam. I believe he may be the same Sam that Pierre knows. What was that about?" I ask Ashton. I can tell Pierre is curious too.

"Pierre, do you know a Sam Howard?" Ashton asks.

"Yes. I have a client. Actually, I think he is an agent," Pierre says.

"Does he know Jake?" Ashton looks like he's hosting an interrogation. "I know he could have gotten a contact through my contacts."

"I'm not sure. He never mentioned a Jake," Pierre replies honestly.

"Well, if I had to bet on it, I'd say Sam is just as involved in this as Jake is," Ashton admits, "and that is probably because of me."

"What do you mean?" I ask.

"Pierre, Sam was my manager—this was before I knew he would lie, cheat and steal to get what he wants. He's sleazy, sly and will do anything for money," Ashton rolls his eyes to the sky. "Before I figured out this about Sam, I thought he was a decent guy," Ashton says looking a bit anxious.

"Let me go back a little. As you might imagine, it's basically impossible to know Rachael and not believe she should have her own footwear company—she has this burning desire, the talent, and the relationships. She knows almost everyone in the business. Well, a few months ago I joked with Sam about nudging her—I even showed him her designs and ask if he had any connections with you, since you seemed to be the designer she most admired," Ashton says with a strange calmness.

"I see," Pierre responds.

"What?" I say.

"Rachael, I didn't know who he was. Those were the days I trusted him with everything," Ashton replies.

I nod.

"Well, at the time Sam seemed to brush off the idea. He didn't even mention to me your connection with the film we were working on at the time, although maybe he didn't know about it? Anyway, when things got ugly between him and me, Sam must have decided to create this mess. He knew about Rachael's designer dreams, and he knew of Jake—I'd told him all about my college best friend Jake Green and how he learned that I married his ex-fiancé. How Jake had been engaged to Rachael when we met and I didn't know the Jake she was engaged to was him. Jake had told me that it was his Rachael weeks after Rachael and I were married in Vegas," Ashton laughs, "Well, not married in Vegas. He had found out I married his ex-fiancé through the media. It was very hard on him. I thought Sam was a friend and was just sharing what had been going on at the time."

"You knew Jake was my ex?" I screech. "You never told me that!"

"Sorry, Rach. I didn't want my friendship with Jake to damage us," Ashton says as he warmly touches my leg.

I look at Ashton dumbfounded, "But I still don't get why Jake would get involved? I'm a nobody. What's the point of doing this to me? Or for me?" I ask curiously.

"Really? That's what you think? That's not what you are." Pierre replies.

I shake my head in confusion.

"What he means is, Rachael, you're iconic. Beautiful. Sexy. The leading lady of the world. Yes. It's that essence and energy my love!" Ashton exclaims passionately.

"It's beyond being beautiful, charismatic, funny, insightful, and talented. It's because people see the essence inside of you. From the moment I met you in the conference room I felt deeply connected and I'm so grateful for the gift you are," Pierre adds.

I stare at him wondering what Ashton is thinking.

"It's true, baby. You're this bright shining light. Why do you think you are followed all the time?" Ashton adds. "You're that big bright star for everyone. People love you for who you are," Ashton adds.

"That's very kind. And I am finally acknowledging that about me. Thank you. But what I'm asking is, what's the motive? What does Jake get out of this—was he trying to break Ashton and me up? Why would he do anything to benefit me after what I did to him? How does creating a scandal for Ashton help Sam—is it simply revenge? What was it for?" I reply flippantly.

"If I had to guess, I would say that for Sam this is about revenge—creating a scandal to ruin my name," Ashton says. "As for Jake's role, I assume Sam contacted him with the plan, but I'm not sure why Jake would go for it. Maybe he thought he could get back at me and somehow resolve things with you at the same time?"

I nod and smile, "Seems possible."

"Rachael, I would hope by now you don't feel like a victim. And you know you chose this on some unconscious level," Pierre pipes in.

"Yes, I receive that," I reply.

"Look. Let's not make this all okay just to create peace. It's not okay. I'm personally tired of avoiding the conflict. Let's see it for what it is. I mean, cool that it woke you up, Rachael. Cool that you created this relationship with Pierre. But to be perfectly honest, what I see is not okay. So, what energy can we be to create something that will awaken others?" Ashton asks.

"Thank you for that Ashton. I completely agree," Pierre replies.

I smile in agreement and check my phone to see what time it is. I gasp and grandly hold up my phone as I say, "Well, it's time to create something," I smile warmly at them both, "Jake just texted and requested that I meet him at two at a café. I'm sure you'll want to join me. Won't you?"

As we make our way to Pierre's car Ashton says, "So, tell me what happened in Cannes?"

I'm riding shot gun so I look to Pierre to answer his question, "Rachael's designs were selected to be in the Cannes Fashion Festival. It's a special event for fashion and shoe designers," Pierre looks to me to continue.

"Yes. Actually, it was my original college design that

was selected to be in the show. It was very similar to the pair that I found in the hospital when I was rudely awakened to find Jake by my side. Actually, when I saw the shoes in the hospital bag I was delighted and confused and slightly pissed. I had remembered them and thought someone else had created them. Which they did, but I didn't know that. They were made so I would recognize them and believe the fabricated story." I explain to Ashton. "Pierre and I have created a better version of them for the actual Cannes event."

"That is awesome!" Ashton says as he rubs the top of my thigh warmly. "So, give me the story! What happened in Cannes? Did any of your designs win an award? " he asks joyfully.

I stare at him. "Um. We didn't stay for the event. I went running off to find you. We have no idea what happened. I had to be with you. Pierre was kind enough to help me," I sigh, "As soon as I knew I was in this strange altered reality, I had to see you. I had to be with you. I love you."

"My daughters Lucy and Gaby are there to run the show. I'll call Gaby after a while and see what's happening in Cannes," Pierre says.

It's funny, an event that once seemed life-changing has lost all significance. In fact, it's very clear that Pierre is in a similar space as I am. We both see what is without tangling ourselves up emotionally around it.

"What else do you know before we meet Jake?" Ashton asks Pierre, changing the subject.

"Here's what I know from the fabricated story." He's silent for a moment. "Jake told Rachael they were getting a divorce. I'm not sure why if he was hoping to resolve things with her. Maybe he wanted closure more than reconciliation. Maybe it was a way to not be intimate with her, maybe that would be crossing a line for him knowing she was in reality still married to you," he lets out a deep sigh.

"Interesting," I watch Ashton's hands tense and release. "And he has a daughter? What do you know about his daughter?"

"Christina," I add.

"Okay." Ashton says rolling his eyes to the sky as if he's assembling the story pieces, "Um. So, who's Christina's mother?"

Pierre looks to me. "Well, we thought it was me," I offer a nervous giggle. "I don't know who her real mom is."

"Has Jake ever been married?" Ashton asks.

We both give an I-don't-know shoulder lift.

"Well, he's a multi-millionaire, let's Google him. I'm sure his company has a media profile and there's probably a Facebook page too," Ashton adds.

"I'll take that task," I respond pulling out my iPhone.

"So, what else don't I know?" Ashton asks me.

"Um. I saw Katie and her daughter." As soon as the words come out of my mouth I want to say something about Sara and the pregnancy test, but don't dare mention that now. I know Ashton doesn't desire to have children. I can't drop that kind of news in the middle of this mess.

"How is Katie?" Ashton asks.

"Oh, she's fine. Her daughter Aslyn is Christina's age.

We went to her birthday party," I say as Ashton's phone shrills. "Katie's a partner in Jake's firm now."

I find some information on Jake via my iPhone "Jake was married. Yes."

Ashton's phone rings. He looks at the display and says, "Speak of the devil."

He answers, "Sam?" He pauses for Sam to respond, "You're in Paris? Okay. I'll see you soon." He presses the end button on the phone and places it back in his pocket. Ashton's eyes become very wide as he looks at us. "Well, Sam is here too. I'm going to meet him for lunch at Le Café de Paris. Where are you meeting Jake?"

"Same," I reply as I hand Ashton the iPhone to read the article.

Ashton nods, "Oh my. That's crazy." "What?" Pierre asks curiously.

"Amy Sara Green, wife of Jacob Eric Green, JD Born 5-2-1980. Deceased 1-3-2012," reads Ashton. "She had a rare blood disease," Ashton reads. "Pretty girl," he says giving me my iPhone.

I look at the picture and feel a wave of emotions. "I met her once. She went to law school with Jake," I say feeling sorry for her early death.

"Here it is," Pierre announces when we arrive at the café.

As we enter, Pierre greets the door person with a few French words and gestures. I have to admit, I find myself attracted to his kindness both in French and English.

We are seated and I order a cinnamon latte with

whipped cream. Ashton gives me a shocking look regarding my choice.

"Yeah, I've found a few unique tastes while you were gone," I say teasing him. "Or should I say since Silvia's been away."

"No problem. I'm just surprised. I love that you are becoming free from Silvia's restricted nutrition rules," Ashton grins back.

"Look," Pierre points to the door.

"What's she doing here?" I say as both Jake and Katie walk to the table.

"Hi Rachael, Ashton," Katie nods to each of us individually. "Hi Pierre, I wasn't expecting you. I'm so happy to meet."

"Hi Katie," I say pleasantly.

"I guess by now it's no surprise that I'm a part of this too," Katie looks at Ashton remorsefully.

"Let's wait for Sam to join us before we get started," Jake kindly says to Ashton as he sits back in his chair cross-armed.

Ashton gives a stern stare at Jake.

"Hello Jake," Pierre says shaking Jake's hand.

I have to admit everyone is a little too relaxed for my taste. Not that I'm expecting a fight, but I expect Ashton to say it like he sees it. Isn't abduction and identity thieving illegal?

"Hello Pierre. I hear good things are happening with the new line," Jake says making small talk.

"Yes. They are. Thanks," Pierre kindly replies.

Ashton looks at me in a way that allows me to know everything's okay. When he gives me that look, I trust him.

Jake nods at the entrance doors and we see Sam walking towards the table.

"Pull up a chair," Jake says to Sam. Sam places the chair between Jake and Katie—probably to protect himself from Ashton.

"Ashton, I'm really sorry about the post," Sam says genuinely to Ashton.

"Cut the crap, Sam! What's going on? I know this mess is one hundred percent your fault. You were my manager, my friend and my right hand man. You know my reputation. My image. My persona. Why? Why do this to us? Is this revenge for breaking our contract?" Ashton speaks with a power—and honestly I have to say I find it rather sexy.

Jake stands breaking up the energetic fight. "Ashton, look, you should be mad at me, not Sam, and certainly not Katie; she was just playing along for my sake."

Ashton nods for him to continue

"Really it's my fault. It was Sam's idea, but I paid for everything. I paid them all off so I could resolve feelings with Rachael. It was selfish." Jake takes a breath. "I'm not trying to win Rachael back. I'm trying to find some sense of peace and fulfillment in my life again." He pauses and straightens his shirt, "Let's just say there has been zero peace in my life since Rachael left. I tried to fill the hole with a dear friend, and almost ruined that friendship," he glances at Katie. "Then focused on money, cars, whatever I could think to try. I got married to a wonderful woman and became an instant step-dad, and even that wasn't enough to provide me with closure and allow me to focus on the present," he sighs.

Ashton nods to confirm he's listening.

"Then my wife died unexpectedly—and before she passed, she told me that she had one regret—that she wished she would have gone after the dreams she'd had for herself while she had the chance. It really hurt when I looked at my life. I realized that I needed to do what it took to see if there was any change with Rachael, to find closure. My intention was selfish. And the love and kindness Rachael has shown me in these past five weeks have healed me and changed me in a way I never knew was possible." A tear tumbles down his cheek.

"But how could you have gone along with this? You didn't think that would be unkind to me—your friend? You didn't see the impact it could have on my career, let alone my marriage?" Ashton asks.

"Yes, but I was so hurt I didn't care. I'm sorry, but the way Sam presented it to me, I thought that although it might damage you, it could really help the rest of us," Jake replies.

"Whatever!" Ashton says with an anger that seems like he might throw something.

"I thought you'd be happy with the results," Jake says.

"Why on earth would it make me happy?" Ashton replies at little less angry now.

Kate reaches for Jake's hand.

"I'm sorry. I'm not so sure how this abduction makes things better for you, Jake. It's obvious that Sam got revenge."

Ashton replies with a steely look in Sam's direction. I think I can actually see anger flames coming from Ashton's head. "Rachael is now part of an amazing business, but it nearly cost her her sanity," he adds. "But you are still without Rachael and now part of a publicity scandal."

"I know I didn't fully think through all of the repercussions this would bring," Jake explains, "but I was looking for resolution and peace. And I found it. It was Rachael that allowed me to stop looking for it outside myself. Together we've both changed," Jake looks to me and continues.

"I don't know what to say, Jake, you should have asked me. I could have arranged for you to resolve your feelings with my wife," Ashton spouts venom to Jake then looks to Sam ready to spout more. "It didn't have to be done behind my back. You could have included me. Was this why the film was set up in a remote location? Sam? Don't you think there is something underhanded and wrong with that?" Ashton screeches.

"So. Now what?" Ashton speaks with a potency. "Sam, you got back at me. Jake, you're resolved. Kate, you got your friend back. Pierre, you got a new creative designer. Rachael, you have your dream job and seem truly happier. And I got a joyful wife. So, where do we go from here? And what do we need to tell the public? What needs to happen now?" Ashton asks in his professional voice.

"There's something else, Ashton," Jake says.

"Yes. We have a plan," Sam responds.

231

"I'm listening," Ashton says defensively.

"Well, we recorded everything," Sam says in one quick statement.

"The answer is no. Don't go there, Sam," Ashton responds.

"How could that help us?" I ask quietly.

"We filmed it all and it's been professionally edited giving Rachael the star leading role. We can release it as a film. We'll need your approval to move forward of course," Sam responds.

I look to Ashton for interpretation.

"He's saying they've created a film from your little adventure and we can allow it to be released to theaters if we choose." Ashton says in dismay.

"No way. No!" I screech in horror.

"Actually Rachael, it puts you and Sinder Ella Soles in a very beautiful light. I was a part of the editing. I had your back and it would be huge for your shoe company," Jake says.

"It's not my company. Remember?! I was just a pretend partner," I say in a snotty childish tone.

"Of course it is your company, Rachael," Pierre says warmly. "Sinder Ella Soles are made of your designs, your creativity, your essence. And a part of the agreement was if everything worked out, I would make our partnership official. You can thank Jake for that."

"Really? Yay! Thank you Jake," I jump up and give Pierre a big hug. "Thank you! Wow! Oh my goodness. Thank you so much."

"That's fantastic!" Ashton adds.

"Congratulations," Kate pipes in.

"Rachael, you should see the film. You'll love it. We've arranged a private screening for you and Ashton. Of course, Pierre is welcome as well," Jake interrupts.

"Okay. When can we see the edited footage? I mean if Rachael says it's okay," Ashton asks. I can tell he's curious.

"Tonight actually. You are going to love it. We've arranged something pretty special for you," Sam says with delight.

"I'll believe it when I see it. And nothing will be released until we see and edit it to our approval," Ashton responds.

"Ashton, give it a chance. Please." Sam pleads.

"I will, but what you did is inexcusable and unacceptable. I'm not putting my life on display unless it will change lives and it portrays Rachael in an extremely beautiful light," Ashton exclaims.

"Ashton, you should know we presented this as if she was the star actress. No one will know that it wasn't an act. They won't know it's a manipulated reality. They won't see her as a victim and they will see what she was doing with Jake as an on-set and in-character experience," Sam says convincingly.

"Oh. I see. This is your way to save the day—or to make some extra money as you enact your revenge," Ashton responds.

"It would clear you both from this delusional activity if the public is told the reason Rachael was with Jake and

Pierre while you were gone was because she was creating a film," Sam says convincingly.

"No, Sam. This is just a tool to exploit us further. It's not worth it," Ashton yells.

I look at Ashton and with confidence say, "Ashton, let's give it a chance. Okay? This might open the door to other possibilities. Let's see what's possible instead of closing the door with all these conclusions. Are you game?"

"I'm open to see the private screening if you want to. We can make other decisions from there. But Rachael, it's important that you want this. You decide," Ashton finally agrees.

25

It Is... What It Is

WE ARRIVE AT A PARISIAN theatre thirty minutes early. I'm wearing a new daffodil chiffon dress that we purchased earlier in the day. We are greeted at the door by Sam and he directs us to be seated anywhere we desire.

We sit. Ashton and I exchange glances as the lights dim. "This better be good," he whispers to me.

"It better be amazing," I whisper into his ear and he squeezes my hand with acknowledgment.

The film starts with Jake, Sam and Kate sitting in Jake's living room. They are talking about the intervention and the premise: What if one day you had a fall and woke up with a different life? Would you be different? Would it awaken you? An emotional cocktail of anxiety, anger and excitement are brewing inside me. I can tell Ashton feels the same as he squeezes my hand in acknowledgment and love. I watch as Sam says to Jake and Kate, "If we could demonstrate the processes and tools of true transformation we'd help millions awaken and embrace change for the better." They are now showing Ashton at the premiere attempting to convince me to go to Fiji with him once again. It seems different now. He was so real and loving. He really wanted me to go with him. For some reason I perceived it totally different. Wow. I really have changed. I really have stopped the cycle of resisting and reacting to everyone and everything. Of course this segment ends with me falling and being taken to the hospital. It's interesting to see yourself unconscious on a stretcher, but I actually look pretty good despite my rain drenched clothes. Ha. Ha. It is funny when I try to surprise no one when I first walk into Jake's house. Then with a grip, suddenly, I remember the clatter in the bedroom with Pierre the day I came home sick. I knew that was a camera clank noise. Now they are showing the discovery of the journal and my high alert states. Yikes. I see my naked body falling into Jake. That was filmed very nicely. I look at Ashton. He's laughing hysterically. That's a relief. The shock on my face when I am told to draw the Hilton sandals is priceless. Funny. Wow. I've really grown in a few weeks. The edits really bring out the best in me. You can see my joy, bliss and light. Yay! Oh Kate's Party. Here we go. We see the fight and conversation about the kiss with Jake. And then the bathroom slash pregnancy reveal is in there. Ashton gasps when Kate's friend finds the test in the trash. Then we watch the car accident and how I start to gain a deeper connection with Jake. I look at Ashton while I'm dancing with Pierre at the charity ball—he seems impressed. The film finishes with the meet up at the tower and even the proposal. I gasp when Ashton proposes as if I've just experienced it.

As the credits reel, I look at Ashton who's grinning from ear to ear. I am happy to see it's not about the drama of me, but it's about the essences of the true me.

Once the lights come on I see Pierre and Sam standing at the back door. Sam comes in and warmly says, "Thank you. Thank you for your willingness, Ashton."

I personally find myself being overtaken with joy. I love being the star.

I snap back when Sam says, "Now, let me personally congratulate the happy couple on their engagement. Ha, so much for Vegas weddings, right? You two are made for each other. Congratulations." Then Sam grandly turns to Ashton and says, "So, what do you think about the film?"

"It's really good. I don't appreciate what you did to us to get the footage, but the film is good," he tells Sam. "Rachael, what do you think?"

"I love it. I've always wanted to be the star," I reply.

"Fantastic! I do think this will resolve things, hopefully between us as well, Ashton? Rachael, you are a star. I'm glad I could bring that out in you," Sam replies with an animation I've never seen from this straight-laced guy.

Ashton says to Sam, "I would concur with that."

"I have one question," Ashton starts, "Why the scene with the pregnancy stick? What's that about? The editing seems to suggest it's Rachael's—or was it supposed to be Kate's?"

I drop my head back and laugh as I don't know what else to do.

237

Pierre pipes in, "Ashton, that's real. Were you two trying?"

"We were hoping to add something in the film that clarified that, but we never received footage of Rachael telling you," Sam says.

My stomach gives a little flip as I watch Ashton turn his eyes to meet mine. He finally says, "Well, it's a good thing we are getting married. Isn't it, baby?"

My body relaxes and I reply with a simple, "Yes, it is."

26

Infinite Love and Gratitude

FIVE WEEKS LATER, I'M SITTING at my dressing table in our LA home. Katie is behind me putting on my tiara and veil. My dress with its embroidered silk cleavage-enhancing bodice fits perfectly around my expanding figure.

"Rachael!" says Katie shakily, "You are beautiful." Her eyes are tear-filled as she looks away.

"Thanks," I say fluffing the chiffon train. "I'm so pleased with the couturier's work!"

"I mean, you are really beautiful. You are a beautiful person, a genuine friend and full of pure joy. In college it never seemed that you cared about anyone but yourself. But now, you're completely different. You would walk through fire for those you love. I feel so grateful to have you back in my life as my best friend," Katie says.

"Don't make me cry. I don't want my mascara to run." I reply playfully as I turn and give her a hug.

"I'm sorry," Katie says looking at Jake who just poked his head into the bedroom.

"We're ready," Jake says.

"Ready?" Katie asks me.

"Yes. I'm so ready," I smile.

As we step out of the room I hear the wedding music playing in the background, the florist hands me a sterling rose bouquet and my two flowers girls receive a silver basket of sterling rose pedals. I receive them with a wave of intense emotions.

I'm sure *In Style* magazine will print something about me and my running mascara, but I don't care—it will be what it will be. And maybe they will print something about Sinder Ella and my designer soles. We can always use the exposure.

Once I arrive next to Ashton my overwhelming emotions become intense luscious tingles of love. I hand Katie my bouquet and I catch a glimpse of Jake and Pierre's smiling faces in the front rows. I turn to Ashton and see his eyes move from my footwear to my face.

"Now those heels are a gateway through my body and my infinite being," Ashton whispers.

I smile as a true feeling of infinite love and gratitude flows through all of me.

The minister reads and our rings are exchanged. Finally, he says, "You may now kiss the bride." We embrace and we are now officially married.

27

Six and a Half Months Later

I'M SITTING ACROSS FROM Ashton at the kitchen table with three footwear sketches in front of me. He's eating eggs and reading the paper. I sit there contemplating which one to create for the Sinder Ella Soles line. I scribble a few side notes.

Then finally I push them in front of him. "So, what do you think? Do you like the one with the decorative clip or without, or this one?" I point to the third sketch

Ashton scoots his chair to my side, "The relationship between one and one's footwear is very personal and intimate."

"Yes." I nod.

"They inspire our dreams," Ashton smiles.

"Yes," I nod almost hypnotically.

"They belong in a loving relationship with trust and respect."

"Yes." I nod again.

"They have to be present with all things and engaged in each step of life. Even those first steps that require a ton of courage," Aston adds.

I smile.

"They have to move you."

"Ah. Huh." I giggle.

"And they must reveal the magic within the wearer." His face is all lit up. "And if the wearer does not acknowledge the magic they will be humbly put in their place."

"Yes." I reply humbly choking back emotions when I realize he is talking about himself.

He reaches over to bring me in for a kiss when the baby kicks really hard. "The baby agrees," I drop my head back and laugh.

"Mrs. Hunt, I'm ready for true co-creation and I'm absolutely honored to bring a part of you and me into my world."

"Augh," I grunt with a sudden contraction. And suddenly my water breaks and I stand there stunned.

"Well, let the magic begin," Ashton laughs.

28

Twenty-Four Hours Later

I CAN'T BELIEVE I did it. I'm officially a mommy—for real this time. I just brought the most gorgeous daughter into the world. She has brown hair and blue eyes. I'm surrounded by friends. Ashton is on my right, and Katie and Jake are on my left. Katie is holding Cynthia Ella right now. I watch as she kisses her tiny little feet and she giggles with delight. It's a dream come true. I look up and say, "Thank you for my fairy tale ending."

About the Author

Jeneth Blackert has fast become regarded as The Change Agent. She playfully invites people around the globe to open to greater oneness and possibility. With a background in corporate blended with her very unique approach to change, Jeneth has an ability to profoundly deepen her client's lifestyles. Jeneth runs a 7-figure conscious-based change agency with programs, products and events designed to expand possibilities.

Jeneth has also been on many well-known television and radio shows worldwide including Martha Stewart Radio, NPR, Fox News and hundreds of radio acronyms around the nation. Find Jeneth online and receive a free training at: www.jeneth.com

CPSIA information can be obtained at www.ICGtesting.com
Printed in the USA
BVOW03s0938301013

335030BV00011B/189/P